Wolf Town

Bridget Essex

Rose + Star Press

Books by Bridget Essex

A Knight to Remember
Dark Angel
Big, Bad Wolf
The Protector (Lone Wolf, Book 1)
Meeting Eternity: The Sullivan Vampires, Vol. 1

About the Author

My name is Bridget Essex, and I've been writing about vampires for almost two decades. I'm influenced most by classic vampires– the vision of CARMILLA (it's one of the oldest lesbian novels!) and DRACULA. My vampires have always been kind of traditional (powerful), but with the added self-torture of regret and the human touch of guilt.

I have a vast collection of knitting needles and teacups, and like to listen to classical music when I write. My first date with my wife was strolling in a garden, so it's safe to say I'm a bit old fashioned. I have a black cat I love very much, and a brown dog who actually convinces me to go outside. When I'm actually outside, I begin to realize that writing isn't all there is to life. Just most of it! I'm married to the love of my life, author Natalie Vivien.

The love story of the beautiful but tragic vampire Kane Sullivan and her sweetheart Rose Clyde is my magnum opus, and I'm thrilled to share it with you in *The Sullivan Vampires* series, published by **Rose and Star Press**! Find out more at **www.LesbianRomance.org** and **http://BridgetEssex.Wordpress.com**

Bridget Essex

ISBN: 1500848328
ISBN-13: 978-1500848323

Wolf Town

DEDICATION

To Natalie–I wrote this book the month we were married. You are just like magic, and every day spent with you is enchanting. Thank you for sharing this journey with me. I love you.

And this book is especially dedicated to Terri, whose incredible support, kindness and good humor always inspire me to tell more stories. This wolf's for you, my friend!

Chapter 1: The Vision

My mother named me Amethyst Stardancer Linden, because she wanted me to grow up to be a witch like her. She got her wish, and I got a weird name.

One of the upsides of being a witch? Lots of holidays. Right now it was Mabon, which, I suppose, if you're a non-witch person, you would call the end of September. Mabon is one of the high holy Sabbats in witchcraft: the coven gathers together and does rituals of gratitude and eats things like oat cakes and Love Potion Stew (my mother's recipe), and Sandy inevitably gets into the rum, and Emily talks about her ex-husband a lot, and Tammie ends up on the living room floor, trying to hear the spirits speak to her.

In other words, it was just a totally normal day in my mom's house. Or, at least, it *would* have been a totally normal if we weren't having The Argument—for the twelve millionth time this week.

"You can't move," said Mom, brandishing about her wine glass filled with grape juice. She never drinks on Sabbats, because she says the alcohol makes her feel less focused on the magick at hand. Sandy vehemently disagrees with that philosophy—and always drinks double.

"*Mom*," I said, dragging out the syllable with a sigh, "we have been over this *literally* —"

"Moving? Our Amethyst *moving*?" That's Nancy. Mom's best friend, coven leader, head librarian and founder of the East Lionsville Feminist Committee. She talks about rituals in empowerment terms and invokes Susan B. Anthony's ghost when asked to name her personal Goddess. "Sweetheart, it's about time," she said, leaning over the table and patting my shoulder. "I was wondering when you'd grow some ovaries. I mean, you're *thirty* and living in your mother's house…" She tut-tutted and gave me a judgmental smile.

I shook my head and rolled my eyes, though I cringed inside. I was already painfully aware that living with my mother at the age of thirty *kind* of made me look like a loser to the rest of society. "Thanks, Nan," I groaned.

"No, I'm serious! Katherine," Nan said, turning to my mom and punctuating her words with a finger stabbing at the sky. "You're stunting her growth by letting her live with you. She has to set sail into the great wide world. She has to—"

"—stay until she decides what she wants to do with her life," said Mom firmly, shaking her head. "She has no clue! It's perfectly lovely having a grocery store job, and that gives her a chance to figure out her life, make the right choices!"

"Look at me, standing right next to you, where I can hear every word you're saying." I smiled tiredly and cocked my head to the side.

"Sweetheart. Another six months. Decide your life path, and then seize it." Mom put her arm around my shoulder and steered me toward the living room. She's not really that dismissive; mostly, she listens. But the last time I brought up the fact that life in East Lionsville was sort of stifling me, she'd finally begun to realize that I was serious about leaving. Not just her house, but leaving East Lionsville for good.

Still, she was right. The matriarch of East Lionsville was *always* right. I didn't know what I wanted to do with my life, had stayed in college until they'd practically kicked me out. I was tired of academics, and I had been at the grocery store job my mom just mentioned for about six months now. Six months, and I still had no clue what I wanted to be when I "grew up," and—news flash—I'd grown up a long while ago. I'd almost been diagnosed with a lifetime miasma.

For heaven's sake, how difficult *was* it to find an open-minded girlfriend in East Lionsville who wouldn't hightail it away when she found out that her lover was a witch?

Answer: really, really difficult. And one

of the major reasons I had to leave.

East Lionsville had a grand total of three resident lesbians: Mandy Patter, who I'd dated in my first year of high school, and who had later decided she only liked the boyish girls (and who may or may not have broken my heart); Katie Donaldson, who I'd dated my entire senior year of high school, and who had had a terrible obsession with college football; and Carrie Bernard, who had just recently dumped me for Mandy Patter (who had promptly decided that ladylike ladies may be her taste, after all). So I'd pretty much run out of romantic options.

I just needed to leave.

I'd spent my entire life in this tiny town: I knew every crack in the sidewalk, every man, woman and child, and I was desperate for something…well, something I couldn't even name.

I didn't have a plan. I just knew it was time for me to go.

Mom directed me into the living room, where the round coffee table had been dragged into the center, draped with a bright purple cloth, thusly transforming it into Ye Olde Sacred Space — otherwise known as an altar. Mom angled me to sit on the couch, and then she bustled about, removing the family pentacle from our ancestor shrine, placing and lighting a dangerous number of candles about as she chattered with the various coven members, who began to join us.

As I sat on the couch, and as I listened to the women murmur and chuckle, I felt the energy shift, and I knew how much I would miss this. I'd been raised as a witch, had partaken in every Sabbat from the time that I could stand on my own tiny feet. I remembered my first Lammas, my first Litha, could feel the pull of the wheel of the year down to Samhain— Halloween. I would miss my mother's sure voice invoking the Goddess, would miss the warm, worn hands that clasped mine as we formed the circle, would miss the cloying scent of sandalwood and patchouli that my mother insisted was the most sacred of incenses (I always preferred dragon's blood, myself). As I stood, as the ladies began to form the circle, Nancy clasping my right hand, Mom my left, I closed my eyes, breathed deeply, and felt my heart beat slower, felt time shift and slow.

And I knew that this was going to be my last Sabbat at home.

It was this deep certainty that climbed up my spine, settling at last behind my ribs, coiled, expectant and waiting. As I stood more firmly, feet solid against the floor, standing straighter, grasping tighter to the hands connecting me to the circle, something odd happened. I'd seen visions before, had dreams that came true. It wasn't odd for me to have a glimpse of something important in ritual. I mean, my entire family had the Gift—with a capital "G." But I'd never been gripped by it so fiercely, or so suddenly.

I opened my eyes, and I saw myself standing on a street corner I didn't recognize. I looked happy, hands jammed into the pockets of my favorite red coat. Actually, I didn't just look *happy*; I was grinning like a *fool*, had, in fact, a ridiculously sappy expression illuminating my face. I crossed the street (may I point out that I didn't even look both ways?) and fumbled with my keys at the lock of the bright purple door of an old store. The sign over the shop read "Witch Way Cafe."

I turned, in the vision, and the grin that broke over my face couldn't even accurately be described as cheesy. It was a whole cheese *factory*. And then there was a rush, and my heart began to pound: a woman came into the vision and put her arms around my waist with a possessiveness I'd never experienced before. She had bright red hair that framed her face in cascading waves, and green eyes that flashed expectantly. She wore a crooked grin, and when she leaned in and kissed me, my toes actually curled in my boots. It was so wonderful. So perfect. So utterly…magical.

"Amy?" The vision evaporated in front of me, and my mother was shaking my arm, calling my name. There was a slight murmur around me, and I realized that I was sitting on the edge of the couch, back poker straight, mouth open.

"Hi," I said quietly to Mom, blinking once, twice. I felt spacey, as if I'd just downed way too much coffee—which I was prone to do.

"Honey, did you see anything?" That was Nancy again, ever ecstatic to see her favorite "niece" exercise her gift.

I blinked for a long moment before nodding, my brows furrowed. "Um, yeah," I muttered, running a hand through my hair and leaning back against the couch. "Huh. Um..."

"Don't talk yet!" bellowed Nancy, holding up her arms. "*Sit* with the feeling, sweetheart."

"Oh, Nan, she's sat with it long enough," muttered Mom with a roll of her eyes. "What was it, sweetheart?"

I didn't quite know how to describe it. The vision... Was it really a vision? Something strange had just happened, I realized. Something strange and special.

I brushed my fingers over my lips.

I had never been kissed like that, not in real life. And, in that moment, I wanted it more than anything else.

There had been two words whispered into my ear, right before my mom called me back. Was it the Goddess, or was it a ghost, or was it my future self, whispering a promise? I went over all of the witchy possibilities, and then the New Age ones, and finally considered the mundane explanations. I decided that the voice was probably my higher self, with a pinch of the Goddess, which is a believable magical equation. Not that it even mattered where I'd heard it from. It pulled me now, a directive from fate, a compass spinning and ending at a point, straight and true.

The words had spelled a village, up the coast, one I'd only heard of in passing.

Wolf Town.

"Um," I cleared my throat. "I saw...a woman..." I began, biting my lip.

"Woman?" all the women gathered together muttered amongst themselves.

"I made out with her," I told them helpfully.

"A sign!" Nan pronounced as my mother looked at me with narrowed eyes, the gears in her head turning.

"Was that it, sweetheart?" Mom asked me again.

"Well, no, someone said 'Wolf Town,'" I told them, clearing my throat.

My mother blinked at the same moment that Nan leaned down and said, "You have to leave right away. Next week!"

"Now, wait a minute," my mother began, but I was staring at Nan, who'd just drawn a letter out my mother's pocket, sneaking her hand into the billowing recesses of my mother's purple ritual robe.

"See, Katherine, I *told* you," said Nan breezily, waving the envelope under my mother's nose. "Things have a habit of taking care of themselves, don't they?"

"What are you talking about?" I pressed, leaning forward slightly as Nan and my mother locked gazes, their eyes flashing in a secret power struggle.

As much as I loved them, sometimes they still treated me like a kid. Even though I was past thirty.

"Well," said my mother then, drawing out the single syllable until it took about a full minute to say. "Your aunt lives in Wolf Town."

"Which aunt?" I managed, despite my surprise, gazing around the room and spotting three of my mother's sisters right here. She had a *lot* of sisters, though.

"Aunt Bette," said my mother briskly.

Aunt Bette? How come I'd never heard of Aunt Bette? In our closeknit family, I knew every third cousin twice removed. How could the existence of an aunt have escaped me? But I didn't have time to question my mother further. She was standing, smoothing the wrinkles out of the front of her ritual robe as her eyes narrowed again, and she told me noncommittally, "She runs a café in Wolf Town, and she seems to be in need of, uh—a vacation."

A scene from my vision flashed across my eyes. "Is it the Witch Way Café?" I asked weakly.

Everyone in the circle stared at me.

"Yes," said my mother, with brows raised. Lips pursed, she shared another very meaningful glance with Nancy.

"Hey, I'm right here, remember?" I told them quietly, waving my hand.

"Your aunt needs a vacation, dear," said Nancy kindly then, sitting down next to me and grapsing both of my hands, as if she was about to do a tarot reading for me. "She's owned the Witch Way Café for a...very long time. And she works very hard. She never gets to take a break. And she wrote your mother asking if one of us could come up and watch the café while she went away for a little while. It's a small café. It doesn't get many visitors, and Wolf Town is pretty small, too. Does that sound like something you'd like to do? Tend the café for maybe..." She glanced up at my mother, cocked her head to the side. "Maybe a month?"

I bit my lip. I didn't even think about it. I needed a change of pace *yesterday*. Though Wolf Town didn't exactly sound like a bustling metropolis, maybe it could provide the change of pace I needed. "Sure," I told them all.

"Okay, then," said my mother, running a hand through her hair. "That settles it. It's meant to be."

The women around the circle nodded sagely to each other as I watched them, feeling utterly mystified.

When the ritual was over and the coven members had stuffed themselves at our Mabon feast (Mabon is our Thanksgiving, so it was a big spread, complete with a turkey, stuffing and about a million squashes cooked in different ways), our house emptied out, and I watched as my mother made her way up to the hallway closet.

Everyone had been acting pretty weird since my vision, so I followed Mom upstairs, a hundred questions hovering on the tip of my tongue. When she reached the hall closet, she pulled her old suitcases out of it, dragged them into my bedroom, and began loading them up with my books.

"Mom?" I said, brows narrowed.

"Honey, when a vision comes from the Goddess, we listen," she said, tossing *The Hobbit* into the case.

I was about to bring up the fact that she had been staunchly opposed to my moving for *forever*, but this was what I had wanted for a long time now, and I didn't want her to go back to arguing that I should stay.

Still, kind of weird that my mother was so gung-ho about my impending exodus all of the sudden. "Meant to be," she'd said. Could I chalk that up to the Goddess' mysterious ways, or was Mom's flinching and haunted look that lasted about five minutes after I brought up Wolf

Town an indication that there was more to this change of heart than met the eye?

I filed that one away for later ponderings.

The days passed and the weekend flew by. My mother spent a little time in hushed conversation on the phone, assumedly to my new aunt—Aunt Bette—who I'd never known existed. I felt that, somehow, I should be questioning that omisson, but there's a lot of mystery in witchcraft, and honestly? I was too excited about the prospect of experiencing something new and fresh to really wonder what my mother was up to.

Monday morning dawned gray and foggy, the perfect setting for the beginning of a quest. Mom helped me put the boxes in the Subaru, and—when there were no more boxes to load—leaned against the passenger door, folded her arms, and sighed a lot.

"Well," I said, playing with the car keys. What does one say in situations like this? "I guess this is...it."

"You know," said Mom quietly, seriously, "if I wasn't a witch, I don't think I could do this. I just *know* you're going to be okay. I had a dream about you last night..." She adjusted my headband, carefully avoiding my eyes. Her own eyes were watery. "I had a dream that you met a real nice girl."

"Thanks, Mom," I said, alarmed at how my voice cracked. I absolutely, positively couldn't cry.

"Do you know the stories about Wolf Town?" she asked then, looking me in the eyes this time. She rubbed at face with her shirtsleeve. I shook my head.

"Good," she said, and kissed me on my brow.

Okay... That didn't sound ominous at *all*.

"Mom?" I asked, as she began to walk up the path, toward the front door.

"Good luck, brightest blessings, may the Goddess watch over you until we meet again, my darling!" She blew me a kiss, and I knew she was crying, then, could see the tears gliding over her cheeks. " I love you!"

"I love you, too..."

I drove to Wolf Town in silence. I cried twice. After the second time, I felt better, lighter almost, as if I'd spent my tears. I was thirty years old. It was well past time to leave the nest, and even beyond that, it was well past time to leave the bigger nest of that tiny town. It was time to follow my heart. It was time for a billion other clichés, because I was driving up the coast in my little Subaru, burdened with a few boxes of belongings and the absolute, distinct hint of *awesome* in the air.

I was driving to a town I'd only heard of, never seen, to begin and make a new life for myself.

I was a heroine! The mistress of my own

destiny! Invincible!

Had there been a little less singing along to rock anthems and a little more paying attention to my surroundings, I might have noticed the sign when I entered Wolf Town. As it was, I didn't. But I'd know it, soon enough.

Wolf Town's sign reads like this:

Welcome to Wolf Town.

But it doesn't *actually* read "Wolf Town," because someone sprayed an "x" through the words, and wrote next to it, in big, sharp-looking letters, "the strangest place on earth."

Chapter 2: The Ghost

It was only about noon when I pulled into Wolf Town. It hadn't been nearly as far up the coast as I'd thought; it was pretty close to the shore. My scribbled directions told me my aunt's cafe was on the main drag of town. The town itself looked appropriately New England-y, with flat store and house fronts, each building painted dark blue or brown, with occasional lengths of brick interrupting the crumbling sidewalks. There was a sub shop, and a seafood joint, and a wine store, and a bookstore (thank the ever-living gods), and a coffee shop.

Coffee...

My stomach was rumbling something fierce, and my coffee had dried up about an hour ago. I needed sustenance in the form of an extremely sugary, caffeinated beverage.

The coffee shop was called The Ninth Order, and when I ducked inside, I had to pause for a moment. I'd never seen a coffeehouse so large. It boasted extraordinarily vaulted, churchy ceilings, and went back so far that I'd probably have to shout if I wanted to tell the barista something, since the bar was positioned in the distant corner. Comfortable, beaten-up couches lined the walls, and there were overstuffed chairs in every color of the rainbow that looked so inviting, I was suddenly struck by a desperate longing to crumple up in one.

It was noon on a Monday, but almost all of the seats were filled with people wearing…weird stuff. I think I recognized a costume from Star Wars, and I certainly spotted the uniform for Star Trek once or twice. And a guy in a moonwalking suit.

"Alien convention," said the woman behind me.

I turned and, totally suave, stared at her with my mouth hanging open.

She had bright red hair that draped down to her thighs, the most adorable turned-up nose I'd ever seen in my *life*, and eyes so green that they must have been contact lenses. I'll abstain from regaling you with a description of the precise span of her bosom, but it had been a really long time since I'd gotten laid. We're talking six months.

So I tried — and failed — not to stare.

She was smiling at me with a soft curve to her lips. I noticed that her biceps were a little muscular, and she stood with her feet hip-width apart, as if she owned her space.

I blinked, and my insides turned to literal mush. I was so utterly attracted to her that I didn't know what to do.

Get a grip, Amy. She's probably not gay.

That throught brought me back to reality with a hard, unwelcome jolt.

"Welcome to the Ninth Order!" she said, with a huge grin. I finally registered that she was wearing an apron with the name of the coffeeshop embroidered onto it, next to an arcane-looking star. "Shall I get something started for you?" she offered, after a long moment in which I continued to be speechless.

I never thought I'd had a type. I mean, I'd only known three lesbians in my entire life, so I couldn't really *afford* to have a type.

But I guess Irish-or-possibly-Scottish-warrior-queen was my type, after all.

"I'd like a latte," I said, cursing myself for my wavery voice. "Um. Do you have any fall flavors?"

"Do you like pumpkins?" she asked, leaning closer to me and raising one eyebrow, as if we were sharing a secret.

Pumpkins. Pumpkin-flavored things. Yes, I liked pumpkin flavored things, but judging by the non-responsiveness of my tongue, I was apparently absolutely incapable of giving an intelligent response to the question.

"Morgan, good heavens! Stop flirting with every poor, unsuspecting girl who walks in here!" someone shouted from the coffee bar. "You'd think this was a den of wolves!"

The redheaded woman, Morgan, glanced

up with a crooked, decidedly wolfish smile. I opened and shut my own mouth. Her canines were a little bit more pointed than any I'd ever seen before. No... They were a *lot* more pointed.

That was...odd.

"Come," she said, and took my hand, threading it through her arm so naturally, as if it were normal to walk arm in arm with a stranger across a coffeeshop floor. This close, she smelled of coffee and vanilla and some intoxicating spice underneath all of that that made my face turn toward hers the entire time that we touched. We walked across the vast expanse of the coffeeshop and up to the bar, where an extremely pale man leaned on the counter. His eyes were very dark, his hair was jet black and spiked, and when he smiled, he, too, had very pointy teeth.

"Hello," he said, and straightened, clapping his hands. "What can I make you? You're new here, aren't you? Are you here for the alien convention? You don't *look* like you're here for the alien convention..." He trailed off and raised a black brow.

Morgan slid around the counter and into the bar area. I tore my eyes from her — forcibly — because I needed to stop acting totally *creepy*. "Um. Alien convention? No, I'm not here for an alien convention. I'm, um, taking over my aunt's café while she goes on vacation..." I smile nervously. "The Witch Way Café?"

"You're Bette's niece? You'll be staying here for awhile?" asked Morgan, leaning on the counter. She stared at me intently, eyes narrowing as they slowly, purposefully, raked over my length. I felt myself begin to turn very, very warm as her full lips hitched up at the corners and she smiled deeply. "That's...nice..." she practically purred.

Um. Wow. That was...definitely flirting.

The guy behind the counter was wearing a nametag that read "Victor!!" The two exclamation marks were transformed into a smiley face. He placed his palms on the counter and leaned next to Morgan.

"Your lesbianness is showing," he said to her brightly. She rolled her eyes and pushed off toward the espresso machine with a chuckle.

"Wait, what?" Had I died and gone to the Summerlands? Had I died and been reborn in a perfect world? Had I...died? This was too much. My gaydar was admittedly atrocious, but the hottest woman I had ever seen in my entire life, who attracted me like sugar water attracts hummingbirds, was actually a *lesbian*?

She turned and winked at me.

I thought I was going to faint.

"So! The Witch Way Café!" said "Victor!!" smoothly, mouth opening into a wide grin. "That's wonderful! Bette's needed a vacation for ages." He placed his chin in his hands, head to the side. "Funny, though—I

29

never knew Bette had any other family."

Yeah, I never even knew Bette existed, I thought to myself, as I dug around in my purse for my wallet, which always delighted in hiding itself from me.

"Yeah," I said with an overenthusiastic shrug. I didn't want to immediately launch into the fact that Bette probably wasn't my real aunt, or that my mother was a witch and had a very large, extended witch family. For just two minutes, I wanted to be normal in Wolf Town. "It'll be good to see her," I told him sincerely. Which was true. I was excited about meeting her, about seeing the café where I'd be spending the next month. I was excited about seeing more of Wolf Town.

But, really, right now I was perfectly content to simply see more of Morgan. The woman had her back to me, frothing the milk in the machine. She glanced over her shoulder at me, one brow raised, smiling invitingly.

She was so beautiful.

I took a deep, trembling breath.

"Fabulous!" said Victor loudly. "Well, we're glad you're here. We hope you'll frequent the Ninth Order." Again, that grin with the pointy teeth. I nodded and found my wallet and paid five dollars for something I couldn't even remember ordering. And then I found a seat and sat down. I wanted to put my head in my hands to keep the world from spinning, but instead I leaned back in the chair and stared at the ceiling for a long moment.

Obviously, I'd known there were other lesbians in the world. But *finding* one—in East Lionsville, anyway—had been like finding a unicorn.

Finding one that I was incredibly *attracted* to felt like seeing a unicorn riding a motorcycle.

But when Morgan came to my table and handed me my expensive, fancy drink, I stared at her left hand with deep sadness and gray regret. Because the ring finger on her left hand had a ring on it.

Unicorns riding motorcycles don't stay on the road for very long.

"I hope you like it," she said, crouching smoothly down next to me, staring into my eyes intently. She was so close, and she was acting overly familiar in the most delicious way, placing her hand on my arm... I forgot to breathe. When I remembered to breathe a few moments later, I inhaled her scent: that intoxicating mixture of coffee, vanilla and spice. I thought I smelled sandalwood and amber as an undertone, too, and though I'd never been a fan of the combination before, it seemed sweeter on her, warmer somehow. Lovely.

When she stood and left, my heart was still skipping.

This was ridiculous. I'd never felt so instantly smitten... I took a sip of my latte and was grateful that the milk was scalding; it burned me all the way down. It brought me — painfully — back to reality.

Including the reality that, according to my watch, I'd better get going. My mother had told me that Aunt Bette wanted to get an early start on her vacation, so she planned to just whisk me around and show me how things at the café worked quickly before she left today.

I stood and sighed, casting a glance at all of the happy Trekkies and... Hmm. What do you call a Star Wars fan? A Warrie? Well, they seemed happy, too, and the moonwalking guy had his helmet on the table and was eating a chocolate chip cookie that was almost as *big* as his helmet. As I walked past him and out of the coffeeshop, I kind of did a double-take: there were two tiny nubs sprouting up and out of his hair. Kind of like those things on cartoon alien heads, I guess. Antennae. Neat costume.

Morgan watched me leave the coffeeshop. I could feel her eyes on me — acutely, intensely — until I turned the corner.

The latte was the best one I'd ever had.

The Witch Way Cafe (according to my directions) was just down the street from the coffeeshop, so I walked. The air smelled of wet leaves and an impending storm, mixed with the pumpkin scent of my latte. It was the most perfect, autumnal aroma in the world. The clouds had been threatening rain all morning, and as I made my way over the sidewalk, two fat drops fell down to show starkly against my worn, black sweater.

I felt a chill just then, like the trail of a cold finger along the back of my neck. Not fear, but something bright and pointed, asking me to wake up and pay attention. I looked up, shivers racing over my skin, and I moved my eyes to the right.

There was an older woman standing precariously on one of the tallest rungs of a very old ladder. She was wearing a bright purple sweater, with a skirt in a slightly different purple shade, along with purple-and-black stockings and toe-curled black witch shoes. She was industriously leaning out much farther than she should to maintain the balance of the ladder, and she was applying a fresh coat of (you guessed it) purple paint to the "e" in "Witch Way Café."

I stared up at her with wide eyes. This was the shop I'd seen in my vision, right down to the bright purple door. The woman's hair was piled in a bright white bun on top of her head, and her tongue stuck out of the corner of her mouth in concentration. Until she caught me staring.

"Why, hello!" she exclaimed, glancing down at me from up high. "Can I help you?"

"No, it's all right!" I called out to her, but she had already started climbing down the ladder, which wobbled and rattled beneath her. She was wearing a very wide smile when she finally leapt down fron the last rung. She tucked a stray wisp of white hair behind her ear as she looked me up and down, finally placing her hands on her hips.

"You're a Linden; I can tell," she said, and then she stepped forward and embraced me tightly. She was an entire head shorter than me, but her hug was sincere, and her arms were surprisingly strong. I smiled over her shoulder, hugging her back.

"Aunt Bette?" I asked, and then she nodded, took a step away from me and patted her blouse pocket, from which she removed a thin pair of glasses. These she settled on the bridge of her nose, and she examined me up and down again as her smile grew wider.

"You look just like your mother," she told me proudly, taking my hand and patting it. Then her eyes began to sparkle. "But enough of this mushy crap. I have a plane to catch, and the traffic around Bangor is unsightly during rush hour. Come on, come on—I have so many things to show you!" She turned on her heel and marched purposefully toward the bright purple front door of the store.

I chuckled and followed after her. She didn't look like any of my family members, but she sure as heck acted like them.

"So, the Witch Way Café doesn't get many customers in a day. Just a few regulars," she told me, taking a small key out of her pocket and handing it to me as she opened the door. "I've been in the middle of a remodel, too, which is just..." She sighed, shrugged. "It's been ghastly. If you get bored, please feel free to pick up a paint roller, but you certainly don't have to. Heck, read romance novels. It's just nice of you to be doing this for me."

"I'm not really a romance novel reader," I told her, stepping into the café behind her and blinking curiously. She flicked on all of the lights one by one, and I was greeted by the sight of a strange, in-between kind of space. One of the walls had been half-painted purple, but the rest were bright, stark white. Glancing at my purple-clad aunt, I couldn't imagine how she had survived this long *without* painting every wall her favorite color. There were several small tables leading up to a counter at the back of the room, and there was black-and-white checkered tile beneath our feet. The place looked a little bit like a 'fifties diner.

"Don't like romance novels?" she said, turning on her heel, hands on her hips.

I shrugged, bit my lip. What had my mother told her about me? "Well," I said carefully, eyebrows up, "not *straight* ones."

"But don't they publish lesbian romance

novels, too?" she asked, without missing a single beat.

I smiled in spite of myself. "Yeah, really good ones."

"Great. So read those between customers," she said, nodding as she waved her arm to indicate the café. "Know how to cook?"

"Um, a little," I muttered.

She shoved a menu into my hands and grabbed a wheeled suitcase from behind one of the tables.

"You'll learn, dear," she said with conviction; then she stood up on her toes and brushed her warm lips over my cheek. "The most important thing is to have fun!" she shouted brightly.

And just like that, she was wheeling her suitcase out of the café.

"Wait, what?" I managed, eyes wide. A moment later, I stumbled after her, my head a tangle of confusion. "Where am I going to sleep?"

"In my apartment above the café." She gestured toward the building behind her and glanced down at her watch. "You can go right in and look it over, if you fancy. I'm sorry, but the normal door is being repaired. It's down the alley there. You'll have to go through the café to get up to the apartment for right now, all right?"

"Um...sure," I murmured, taking a step forward. My skin pricked, and as the wind whipped up, drawing the September clouds closer, a little dust devil swept up leaves and danced by the front door. I could practically *feel* the magic in the air as I glanced over my shoulder at the café now.

"Ciao, darling!" said my aunt, and bustled her way across the street toward a tiny bright red SMART car.

I was kind of shocked that her car wasn't purple.

"Bye?" I waved half-heartedly as I watched her bounce behind the wheel and motor down the road.

Then, a little dazed, I turned around and walked back into the café, staring at the half-painted wall, the old, well-scrubbed tables and vintage chairs, the stack of hand-lettered menus.

And, inexplicably, a surge of happiness flooded my heart.

Well... I'd *wanted* a fresh start. And, almost immediately, my aunt had left me in charge. That was an auspicious sign, right?

I took the steps up to the apartment, and the door opened readily, even without the key.

There were antiques everywhere (including an antique carousel horse, of all things, as tall as me and situated against the dining room wall). The entire apartment was purple-walled and rich with possibility. There were vaulted ceilings here, too, like in the café below, and pretty archways leading into the rooms. The graceful curves and lines made me smile. There was exposed brick in the kitchen, and I ran my hand over its rough surface before I returned to the living room and laid down on the plush purple carpeting to stare up at the ceiling—which, of course, had stars painted on it.

I felt...weird. It was good, this weirdness, like I was in a sort of universal flow. What else did I expect to happen? What else did I expect to go right? Is this how the world worked for other witches, stuff turns out awesomely if you just leap and trust?

It was my first day in Wolf Town, and though, admittedly, I had *no* idea what I'd signed up for (or if that woman had even really been my aunt), I hadn't ever been more excited in my life.

Suddenly, there was a sound. Like a cough.

So I sat up.

Across from me, in the corner, a woman sat on the floor. She wore a long, wispy white skirt and an old, tattered blouse, and her eyes were kind of intense. And burning. Her hair was floating around her shoulders in curling white waves, even though she looked like she couldn't have been older than thirty.

She was also see-through.

A ghost.

I breathed out, and slowly (very slowly)

raised my hands, invoking my own energy and spiraling it around myself as I surrounded my body with a circle of light.

The ghost laughed. It wasn't a creepy laugh, but kind of an "oh, darlin', you have no clue" sort of laugh.

Miffed, I narrowed my brows and frowned.

"I promise, you don't have to protect yourself around me." Her voice, inexplicably, came from behind me, but I didn't turn around to look. We were the only beings in the room, and I should have been alert to her long before now. I'd just been too darn happy, I guess. But I should have steeled myself: old houses always have ghosts. It's like some sort of cosmic law, right up there with "never get out of your car if it breaks down in the middle of a night on a deserted country road because bad things *will* happen."

"I won't hurt you. I'm not evil," she said, and sort of floated upright, to a standing position...five inches off the ground. "At least, I don't think I'm evil. I don't *do* anything evil. I mostly just sit in the corner and read the classics. Like *Little Women*." She shrugged and gave me a bright but very see-through smile.

"Hi," I said, voice shaking just a little. "I'm Amethyst... Amy... Sorry." I sighed. "It's just... I've never seen such a distinct apparition before." I couldn't help it: I stared at her with my mouth open, fists clenching and unclenching at my sides.

"Oh," she said, and sort of sat back down. She folded up like a wobbly jello mold. "Did I scare you?"

"No." *Mostly* the truth.

"It's been awhile since I had anyone to talk to. It gets lonely, being a ghost. Though I bet that's what they all say."

"They...don't usually talk to me," I said, thinking back to the times I'd dealt with apparitions in the past. They'd all been of the spookity-spook variety, the ones that needed to be ushered to the light, posthaste—before they, you know, *ate your soul.*

I'd honestly never met a *nice* ghost before. But my intuition was telling me that this one might qualify. Still, I wasn't ready to fully let down my guard.

"I'm Winifred," she said, extending her hand toward me. I didn't take it—mostly because I wouldn't have been able to touch her, since her hand wasn't corporeal. "But you can call me Winnie, if you think that might be easier to remember. I know most of you folk don't use long names anymore." She smiled, and it eased her burning eyes a bit. "Are you going to be living here?" she asked with interest. "What happened to Bette?"

"I'm taking care of the café for Bette for about a month."

"Oh, that *will* be lovely. Bette really did need a vacation." Winnie clapped her hands and folded upright. "You know, I used to own the café. Well, when I owned it, it wasn't a café... It was a shop. I think that was, oh, one hundred years ago...or so. Time is a little fuzzy when you're dead." She shrugged. "My shop was a general store, in fact. Oh, I was so proud of it. I didn't have a husband, you see, and I ran it all by myself. I'm a good roommate," she added randomly, holding her hands open. "I won't spook you. I won't watch you while you use the lavatory. I occasionally have a few other ghosties over for a sort of get-together—a luncheon, we call it—but we keep it down and don't rattle chains or slam doors or stomp about." She sighed and rolled her eyes heavenward. "We've had to work very hard against that negative stigma!"

I laughed a little and smiled at her. I couldn't believe I was actually having this conversation, but I figured I might as well embrace it. "Yeah, I can empathize," I told her sincerely. "Honestly, I have to work against negative stigmas occasionally myself. I'm a witch. And...I'm gay."

"I wondered why you could see me, my darling!" she said, and then she came over, floating around me in a big circle as she gazed at my little pentacle pendant, at the holes in the elbows of my sweater, at my sparkling ballet flats. "Most witches can see ghosts, you know. Hmm, I'm not sure if most gay folks can see ghosts. But, oh, we'll be the best of friends! It's lovely you came!"

So. I was going to share Aunt Bette's apartment with a ghost. A unexpectedly sweet and amusing ghost.

Sure. I could live with that.

Chapter 3: The Wolf

The most important thing about tea is that it must be made with intention.

You begin with tea leaves. Freshly dried, they crumble beneath your fingers with crispness. You can taste them on the back of your tongue, if your fingers touch them long enough, like sweet salt. Then you add herbs, pretty dried flowers that will hang suspended in the water, mint leaves that have curled as they've dried, looking like little boats. Against the silver strainer in the teapot, they resemble bits of hay before you pour the water over them.

But you don't pour the water. Not yet. You add lavender for love and peace, a few of the buds that fall from your fingers, and top it off with rosehips, for sweetness in life. You hold your hands over the herbs and leaves—so small, but so filled with possibility. And then the magic begins.

It comes up through the ground, through your feet, like water through roots, spreading through you and filling you until you can't contain it. Once you've drawn it up, once it's thrumming like a heartbeat, you let it go, in your hands and your fingers, into the tea, into the pot.

And you pour the water over the tea, and the spell is bound.

I made tea for myself the first night I began to finish my aunt's paint job in the cafe. There was a small stack of paint cans along the wall; the color she'd chosen was called "Iris Passions." It was the most beautiful purple I'd ever seen. I finished painting her half-finished wall, and there was probably more paint on me than on the actual wall, but I considered it a good afternoon's work. I made the tea on an electric skillet I'd dragged with me from home and poured it out into my traveling mug (that read "The Witch's Brew!" around its rim in a Halloween-y font. Since I was a witch, it was less cliché and more truth, but still pretty cheese-tastic). I curled my fingers around the warm mug and inhaled the heady aromas of herb and leaf and spell. And then I drank it down, thanking the Goddess as its warmth filled me.

Leaning against a non-wet wall, paint-covered toes curling in happiness, I felt…content.

A knock came at the door. It was too dark outside to really see, and the floodlamps in here were too bright. I stood and made my way to the glass-fronted door and paused about three feet away from it.

That incredibly gorgeous woman from the coffeeshop was standing outside.

Morgan.

She waved at me a little, crooked smile stretching across her face. She pointed to the door handle with her head to the side, and suddenly I snapped out of it. "It" being the apparent spell of bewitchment and speechlessness that seemed to come over me every single time I saw her. I crossed to the door and drew it open.

"Hello!" I said, and then the chill of the air assaulted me, and I realized how cold it was outside. "Please come in. You must be freezing," I told her, backing out of the way.

"Hi—and thanks," she told me, stepping into the cafe. The cold air crept in behind her as I shut the door, and she unbuttoned the top button of her coat.

"Hi," I said, and then remembered I'd already given a greeting, so I fumbled trying to find new, non-hello-related words. "Um. What brings you around here?"

She chuckled warmly as she unbuttoned the rest of her coat. Her fingernails wore bright red polish, a crimson as red as blood. "I saw you painting on the way to my shift this afternoon," she said, stepping forward, her head angled to the side a little as she took my paint-splattered hands into her own cool ones, rubbing her thumb across my skin as my heart started to beat about a trillion thumps per minute. "And you're still at it now," she growled softly, "so I told myself: self, if she's still at it when I get off work, I am *so* going to help her with that. So here I am! I mean, if you don't mind?"

I opened my mouth to say something, and then I didn't quite know what to say, because she was still rubbing her thumb softly across the back of my hand, and I appeared to be under some sort of trance. I cleared my throat and eventually managed to reply, "Sure!" And then, after a moment, I added, "Thank you."

"Well…" She laughed—a deep, throaty chuckle—and stepped back, shrugging out of her coat in one smooth motion. She folded it over her arm, glanced around and set the coat on one of the café tables. She turned to me with her hands on her hips as she raised a single brow, and—again—her gaze raked over my body. "My offer isn't *entirely* without ulterior motives."

I stared at her, my mouth agape. She was flirting with such industrial-strength skills that I knew I was entirely out of my league. I swallowed as I struggled to keep up. "Ulterior motives?" I murmured.

"Well, of course! I'm curious about you," she said, rolling the sleeves of her plaid button-up shirt and snatching one of the brushes. "See, you're fresh meat around here. We rarely get visitors." She eyed one of the half-painted walls and slathered purple onto the edge of her brush from the open paint can. Then she attacked the wall with a broad stroke. "So tell me all about yourself. Are you really Bette's niece? Did you really like my latte?"

"Um..." I laughed at the latte question; then I took a deep breath. Should I be honest? Should I tell her... Oh, why the hell not? She seemed open-minded enough. "Um, I don't know if I'm *really* related to Bette." Morgan glanced at me with her brows raised, and I kept going. "Look, I think I should get something out of the way. I'm a witch, and it seems like Bette lived pretty out of the broom closet, so you probably knew she was one, too. So I might not be *related* so much as my mom is just really close to her and so calls her her sister..." I was mucking this up. What I didn't really say but wanted to say desperately was a*nd, oh, gods, you're really nice, so I hope you don't think I'm a total weirdo.*

She stopped moving to stare at me.

Great. She definitely thought I was a weirdo. Well, sometimes it works out that way. Not everyone reacts to the "w" word with smiles and toasts and inquiries about the best brands of broomsticks.

"A...witch?" And, like Winnie had earlier, Morgan began to circle me. But *unlike* Winnie, the way she stepped (and she did step, not float around like the ghost) was a bit more deliberate, almost...hunting. Like I was prey, or an incredibly interesting sight. I tried not to swallow (or look at her butt in those jeans) as she stared at me with unblinking green eyes, pinning me in place with the force and power of her gaze.

This wasn't what I'd been expecting.

"Yeah. I'm from East Lionsville." I licked my lips; my mouth was suddenly dry. "My mother is Katherine Linden. I don't know if you know of her, but she's kind of a famous witch…" I stalled out. My mom was famous in New Age circles, and for a few psychic television appearances. Most people—non-witch people—hadn't heard of her.

"You're a Linden," said Morgan, and I blinked at the tone of her voice. She'd paused behind me, and when I turned to look at her, her face was unreadable, but she was observing me with an odd expression.

"Yeah," I said, brows furrowed. "You've heard of us?"

"Yes," she said; she licked her lips as she glanced away. "Huh."

Huh?

"What's the matter?" I sighed. "Do you…dislike witchcraft? Tell me you're not a right-wing Bible thumper who thinks I'm going to burn in hell… Gods, I thought this was all going so *well*," I muttered, clutching at my forehead and suddenly feeling very tired.

She laughed then, a bright, friendly laugh.

I stilled, and the tension in my shoulders disappeared like smoke.

"No, no burning in hell," she said. Her smile deepened as she glanced my way with flashing eyes. "I just... What did you say your name was?"

"My name's Amethyst," I said, and stuck out my hand. "Call me Amy."

She entwined her fingers with mine. Now that she had been indoors for a little while, Morgan's skin felt so warm, so soft, and there was such a quiet grace and strength to her: when our fingers met, there was this weird jolt. Like I'd been here, seen this, done this before. *De ja vu* flooded through me, not unpleasantly.

"I wasn't laughing at you," she said then, stepping forward a bit, not letting go of my hand. "I just found the circumstances...amusing." When she smiled again, I noted that her teeth were just as long and sharp as I had thought they were at the coffeeshop. They didn't look exactly normal in a human mouth, poking out beneath her full lips. She tilted her head toward me, a wave of red hair falling sexily in front of one eye. "It's kind of funny, actually. You're a witch," she said breathlessly, her voice a low, throaty growl. "And I'm a werewolf."

"You're..." I stared at her.

"Yeah." She touched the tip of one of her sharp incisors with her tongue. "Definitely a werewolf."

"Okay. Right," I whispered, after a long

beat. I smiled up at her as I chuckled awkwardly. She was a full head taller than I was.

A werewolf...

Granted, the teeth were odd, but was she... She couldn't possibly be serious.

Was she serious?

"Do you mean you're a werewolf in, like, a New Age sort of way?" I asked, backpedaling as my brain began to work as quickly as it could, trying to make sense of her announcement. "So, you, uh, shapeshift on the astral plane and have visions about being a wolf...or something?"

She shook her head slightly as she continued to stare.

Whoa.

Shit.

She was serious.

"You haven't been in Wolf Town long," Morgan growled softly, and her smile was genuine—albeit a bit pointy. "You don't know how, uh, *strange* this place is yet. None of us are 'normal' folk here. In fact, everyone in Wolf Town...we're all a bit...different."

I didn't know what to say, so I bit my lip and blinked a lot.

"Do you believe me?" she asked curiously.

I was a witch. I had experienced many things in my life that a random stranger on the street would never believe had really happened.

I'd sent dark spirits on to the light; I'd used a love spell to get a girl to kiss me once (definitely not recommended, and also *really stupid*); I'd used magic to change streetlights from red to green and find awesome parking spaces and make myself absolutely shiny for that stupid food service interview at a you'll-never-get-me-to-name-it fast food joint. I saw ghosts on a regular basis, had visions that showed me bits of my future, and I believed—absolutely, staunchly, immovably—that the Goddess loved me and helped me out on a daily basis.

Morgan stared at me, waiting. Expectant.

Her teeth were really, *really* pointy. And I *had* heard stories. Rumors. And...hadn't Nancy once told me she'd dated a vampire?

Belief: it's relative.

"I...guess I do," I said carefully, voice low and neutral.

She sighed, an amused smile still slanting over her lips, as she shook her head. "All right, fine, I'll show you. Five seconds... I'm always so stiff after a shift. I have to get better shoes. Better back support." She stepped out of her high heels, and then she began to take her shirt off.

I stared at her with wide eyes, and she paused in breasts-almost-bared territory.

"I hate ruining my clothes," she explained patiently.

My blood was racing through me,

hammering in my head. The sexiest of ladies was undressing in front of me. In my "aunt's" café. With the floodlights on. In front of the really big double windows that showed out easily onto the street.

"Um..." I said articulately, pointing to the out-of-doors. But Morgan shimmied out of her jeans, turned and took off her bra as I stared at her, utterly unable to tear my eyes away.

And then there was a tearing sound, and I couldn't quite tell you *exactly* what happened, because the air sort of shimmered for a moment.

When it stopped shimmering, Morgan was gone.

In the middle of the floor sat a gigantic dog.

I stared, my jaw practically on the ground. No—actually, what was in front of me wasn't a dog. The massive *wolf* licked its lips and yawned hugely, and then it panted, grinning at me. It was black, with a white-tipped coat, and its eyes were so green that they looked bizarre, impossible.

And then, as I watched, the furry snout pushed in, the legs elongated and arms and fingers grew...and then Morgan was sitting exactly where the wolf had been, one arm draped over her breasts and one hand poised in front of her hips, just like that picture of Eve in the garden. Unlike Eve, though, she was grinning like a cat who had just eaten about a dozen canaries. It was a crooked smile that looked utterly sexy and more than a little I-told-you-so.

I sat down quickly on the floor, knees collapsing beneath me.

"You're a..." I coughed, put my hand over my chest, and quickly looked at the half-painted walls, at the black-and-white tiled floor—anywhere but at her beautiful naked body as she rose easily and started pulling on her panties as she chuckled.

"I'm a werewolf!" she said brightly, and drew on her jeans with a wink. She took up her bra and shrugged into it. "It's terrible: these days, you hear 'werewolf' and you think dark, brooding teenager and unexplainable teenage cultural phenomenons. But I promise you," she said, leaning over me in her bra and her jeans and her shirtless-ness. I looked into her eyes and willed my focus to stay there. Which it *sort* of did. "That's not what *real* werewolves are like. My family? We're the MacRue clan, and we've been werewolves for centuries. We came by boat to America. We founded Wolf Town."

She straightened and pulled the shirt over her head, tugging her long hair out of the neck hole and letting it fall over her shoulders in undulating red waves. Her grin was gigantic. And, as previously mentioned, very pointy.

"Wolf Town," she said, and crouched down beside me in one fluid motion, "is bound to surprise you."

"You could say that again..." I whispered, and looked up into her greener-than-green eyes.

Perfectly serious, Morgan growled with a soft smile, "Wolf Town is bound to surprise you."

I laughed in spite of my shock.

She winked and stood, offering her hand to me.

"Thanks for not thinking I'm the hound of Satan!" she said brightly.

"Thanks for not offering to burn me at the stake!" I returned, grinning, as I rose beside her.

So, a werewolf, then.

Sure. Why not?

Chapter 4: The Strange

Werewolves proved to be the norm in Wolf Town. Which, I was finding out, wasn't a normal place at all. It was actually so *far* removed from normal that the address of *normal* might as well have been located in a different country.

Or on a different planet.

The next day, I was woken up by a ghost sitting on me. Winnie's legs were crossed in front of her, Indian-style, and her hair was floating toward the ceiling as she peered down at me curiously. "There's someone at the door!" said Winnie with a wide, see-through smile. "And good morning!"

"I thought we agreed the bedroom was off limits?" I said muzzily to the ceiling, because the resident ghost had already vanished.

I got up, brushed my teeth, peed, drank some water, put on new clothes, ran a brush through my hair, and then—and only then—did I go answer the door, and I felt terrible about taking so long when I saw who it was: an older man with a perplexed expression. He looked apologetic when he took in my half-asleep state.

"Hello. Sorry to wake you so early," he said (the bathroom clock had read eleven thirty, by the way), "but I thought you should know we're having a bit of a water problem and have to shut the water off in, oh..." He looked at his watch. "Five minutes ago, actually. I should probably get headed down there now. You won't have water for the rest of the day, I'm afraid. Sorry about that!" He was already taking off down the stairs. "I'll be back when it's fixed!" he shouted over his shoulder, and then he was out the door.

"That was Burt," said Winnie helpfully, appearing on my right. "He owns this building and an apartment complex, I think. There's trouble in the pipes," she said then, her voice dropping to a whisper. "Bad, bad things in the pipes."

I blinked. I hadn't drunk any coffee yet, so all of this felt like information overload. "What do you mean?" I asked her, frowning.

"There's a *monster* in the pipes," she said, face straight and serious, burning eyes still burning but somehow sympathetic. "Poor little thing. It's stuck something fierce."

"A monster," I repeated slowly. *God*, did I need coffee. "In the water pipes."

"Yes, I saw it!" she said. She seemed as excited as someone (inexplicably) gets at a football game as she clapped her hands delightedly. "I feel bad for the little thing; he is quite cute. He's the son of the lake monster that lives behind Henry's old place."

"Lake monster," I repeated.

Winnie nodded.

I breathed out and tried not to be frustrated, or surprised, or alarmed.

I threw on a hoodie and stuffed my hands into the front pocket. I didn't know whether I should believe Winnie about the monsters or not, but, after all, I *was* having a conversation with a ghost.

So, really, anything was possible.

"You should go tell poor Burt it's a lake monster, so he doesn't do all sorts of unnecessary digging," said Winnie, with a practical wave of her see-through hand.

"Right, I'll do that," I said, and left the apartment with only one objective: the immediate acquisition of coffee. But as fate would have it, when I stepped into the Ninth Order, the guy who'd appeared at my door, Burt, was ordering a coffee to go.

"Didn't even introduce myself. Burt's the name. I take it you're Bette's niece, Amy?" he said, offering a hand to me with a wide smile. I shook his hand with a small smile of my own and nodded. "I've had the darndest time with maintenance this year..." he was saying, but I kind of got distracted by Morgan, who was watching me from behind the counter with one red eyebrow up as she angled me her gorgeous crooked smile.

"I was telling Burt that I think it's the lake monster's offspring again, getting into the well and then the pipes," said Morgan, leaning on the counter, her voice a low growl. "What do *you* think, Amy?"

I blinked.

Burt laughed a little and sighed. "Lake monsters..." he muttered, taking up his to-go coffee cup and leaving as he continued to mutter about excavations and pest control.

Morgan waved a hand after him and leaned toward me a little more, her full lips parted. I swallowed as she licked them slowly and deliberately, sharp teeth bared. "What did I tell you? Wolf Town's a weird place." She pushed off from the counter and straightened, turning toward the espresso maker. "The usual for you, Miss Amy?" The way she said my name made my knees tremble.

I smiled at her. "Do I have a usual?"

"Yes. I never forget a drink," she said resolutely, her voice low as she smiled and began to steam some milk.

"Nice to see you again, Amy!" said Victor, grinning toothily at me as he wiped down the counter. "Morgan was telling me how well you took her werewolf news. Good on you!"

I glanced around with wide eyes, but the place was devoid of alien conventiongoers this morning. I was actually the only person in the place besides Morgan and Victor.

"Uh, thanks?" I said, and coughed a little.

"Hey," he said sympathetically, as he reached across the counter to pat my hand, "no worries. A witch will fit in perfectly here."

His hand was very cold to the touch. Cold...not warm, like Morgan's. I shook my head and laughed a little. "So, lemme guess— you're a vampire?"

Victor laughed, too. "Is it that obvious? Morgan, really, you should remind me when I have to file down my teeth—"

"I'd have to remind you every day, Victor!" She shook her head as she mixed the espresso and milk.

I glanced from Morgan to Victor with wide eyes. Maybe I should have expected vampires, given the helpful, conversational ghost and the too-sexy-for-words werewolf. Still, it's a little surreal.

"There are actually lots of vampires in Wolf Town, from all sorts of different clans. I'm one of the most, heh, *normal* ones we have," Victor said, winking.

"Okaaaay," I said slowly, putting my elbows on the counter. I mean, all of the telltale signs were present (if Hollywood movies are to be believed): Victor had really pointy teeth, a very pale complexion, and his skin was as cold as a Maine winter.

"Um," I began uncertainly, "can you guys tell me how non-'normal' Wolf Town really is? Like, how strange is it *exactly*? So that I don't keep getting the wind knocked out of me..."

Morgan set the paper cup in its sleeve and placed it in front of me. She winked again— long, slow, deliberate. "On the house, darlin'," she murmured softly.

Victor rolled his eyes. "Hey! *I* give out the free lattes around here."

They chuckled for a moment together, but then their expressions became a little more serious as Victor shrugged uncomfortably and Morgan folded her arms, green eyes narrowed.

"Well, you should know that 'strange' is a relative term," said Victor thoughtfully.

"Okay," I tried again. "For example: is there really a lake monster living in the water pipes?"

Morgan cocked her head and considered. "Well, it's a theory," she said thoughtfully. "Ellie has been reproducing like crazy, so one of her offspring could have swum off—"

"Nope. I, for one, think it's one of those mermaids," said Victor, shaking his head. "They wander up the rivers from the ocean, then get lost in the miles of pipes. It's happened before," he added, for my benefit.

"Okay," I repeated; I felt a little lightheaded, but I kept going. "So...are there unicorns?" I asked.

Victor and Morgan looked at one another. Morgan nodded her head a little while Victor shook his.

"There have been rumors," said Morgan, inconclusively.

"Bigfoot?"

"When they migrate, yes," offered Victor.

"Aliens?"

"Absolutely."

"The Easter bunny?"

Victor sighed and shook his head, laughing. "That's just plain mean. We're strange, not creepy."

"Tell you what," said Morgan, leaping over the counter, gesturing toward a comfy-looking couch. "Follow me..."

We both sat down, while Victor busied himself with washing a tray full of already-clean glasses.

"You know what I should do?" Morgan said, leaning forward and brazenly patting my leg. Her hand lingered on my thigh. "I should take you around town, show you all the sights and haunts, give you a bit of local lore... That way, you can see the strange for yourself." Again, that mischievous crooked smile appeared. I loved the way it turned up the corner of her mouth, as if she were imparting an intimate secret. "Does that sound good to you? I'll show you all the weird and wonderful parts of Wolf Town, and you'll fall in love with the place despite — or because of — its weird, wonderful charms?"

I had no idea what I was in for.

But I promised to find out at five.

Her warm palm remained on my thigh. I stared down at it; she still wore a ring on her left-hand ring finger. *Was* she taken? There was a word inscribed on the ring in a tiny font, but it was impossible for me to make out what it said, because Morgan removed her hand and rose with a wide, roguish smile.

"Five," she said, nodding, smiling. "It's a date."

I stared after her as she moved behind the counter. Then I ducked my head to hide the hot blush creeping across my cheeks.

Good heavens, I had it bad.

The only problem with charming, New England, almost-seaside towns is that grocery stores are a little difficult to locate. Grocery stores, in and of themselves, aren't necessarily reknowned for being pretty places. Or rife with charm. They're sprawling megaliths that no New England town wants featured on their main drag, fluorescent lights ruining the small-town ambiance.

Wolf Town proved no exception to this rule. I had to Google where the nearest grocery store was or face starvation—all thanks to time-honored Main Street aesthetics.

And, no, I didn't want to raid my poor aunt's industrial-size refrigerator downstairs. That was for the café. And her own fridge up in the apartment? Yeah, it held a half-empty jar of pickles.

Technically, I probably could have survived the evening on a half-empty jar of pickles. I just wouldn't have enjoyed my dinner much.

The closest grocery store I could find was very, very small. It bore a vintage cartoon of a piglet sprawled over the looping cursive name on the sign. That cartoon pig was more than a little creepy, and I tried not to look at it as I went into the building.

"Welcome to Pig'n'Bucks!" said the greeter guy, handing me a bright blue shopping basket. Despite his exclamation, he didn't appear remotely enthusiastic, but still—this was better service than I'd ever been given in a megalithic supermarket. I wandered down the fresh produce aisle, trying to find sprouts, when I got that pricking little feeling in between my shoulderblades that indicated that someone was probably starin at me.

I turned…

And someone was staring at me.

An older gentleman walked down the grocery store aisle in my direction, pushing a small cart. His hair was gray and carefully combed back from his forehead, and he wore a dark blue sweater and jeans. His eyes crinkled when he smiled, and as he held a wrinkled hand out to me, I realized he looked a little familiar.

"Amy?" he asked when he got closer, and I nodded with a confused frown.

His smile deepened. "I thought that must be you! You're an unfamiliar face here in town, and my daughter's already told me a bit about you. I'm Allen MacRue, Morgan's father."

Ah, yes. *Totally*. That smile was a dead ringer for Morgan's—wide, mischievous, and kind of wolfish.

I smiled back at him and accepted his hand. His clasp was warm and firm, and as we shook with a friendly formality, I considered the fact that I was probably shaking hands with the second werewolf I'd ever met in my life.

"How are you liking our little town?" he asked, with genuine interest.

I replied politely, said some dull things about the weather, the time of year, how beautiful Wolf Town was... His hand—not the one I'd shaken, but his left hand—had a ring on it that reminded me of the ring Morgan wore.

"When my family built Wolf Town, they built it out of a lot of things," he said then, leaning forward, pleasantries done. "It may seem strange to you," he smiled, "but they built it of protection, and they built it of love. And I tell you this" — he raised a finger — "not to bore you with details, my dear, but to explain to you that only the creatures that needed a sanctuary, that *needed* Wolf Town would be permitted to enter, whether they be human, or — well, something else entirely.

"The town itself has always kept out everything bad, everything…intolerant or unkind." He coughed a little into his hand. "I promise you: everyone who came here needed this place. Present company not excepted. Wolf Town takes care of her own," he said, words soft. "She's a very *special* town." There was a forceful tone to his words now, and it made me feel a little uncomfortable.

"Mm," I nodded, as he stared at me, unblinking, his flashing green eyes narrowing to small, bright slits.

"You'll need to ask yourself, in the next little while, Miss Amy, whether you're one of us, really one of us," he said. "Wolf Town's own." He tipped his head to me, said, "Good day," and then he was whistling something just a little out of tune, pushing his cart up the aisle with a strong, confident stride.

I watched him walk away, wiping my hand on my jeans.

I never did find the damn sprouts.

Chapter 5: The Pond

My water was still turned off when I got home, so I pulled my hair up into a ponytail and tried not to worry too much about how I looked (though I did change my shirt—twice), because, really, it didn't matter. There was a ring on Morgan's finger, which meant that she was Totally Taken.

She met me at the café's front door. She smelled of coffee and vanilla, and when she turned toward me, her waterfall of red hair cascading over one shoulder, that spiciness emanated from her, too. The very scent of her made me weak at the knees, and when she smiled at me, my heart somersaulted in my chest.

"Ready?" she asked, her voice growly and so low that I shivered.

"Yeah," I told her.

She inclined her head toward me with a small, wolfish smile and held the door open as we walked out into the cool autumn afternoon. Shoulder to shoulder, we began to stroll down the sidewalk.

"So, let me give you a little history

lesson," she smiled crookedly, looking very, very much like her father. The family resemblance was striking. I'd have to tell her later that I met him.

"Wolf Town," she intoned, gesturing broadly with her arms to encompass the entirety of Main Street, "was founded by the MacRue clan. My family," she said, tilting her head toward me, and then burying her hands deep in her coat pockets. "We came over in the early sixteen hundreds—werewolves, of course—and founded a town where we couldn't be persecuted for being who we were, what we were, openly. So, of course, the town was founded as a sanctuary for the strange, the different, and—because of that reason, I think— it's attracted all sorts of other...oddities."

A gust of wind chose that moment to dance across the twilit streets, kicking up brightly colored leaves in its wake. The sound of their skitter across the pavement, the scent of leaves burning in some nearby backyard and fallen on the sidewalk, filled my senses. Autumn had come to New England, yes, but autumn seemed to have passionately claimed Wolf Town more possessively than anyplace I'd ever experienced before.

"I'm glad you're here," said Morgan then, surprising me. She wasn't looking at me, was glancing down at the sidewalk in front of us, but when I looked over toward her, she met my eyes with her own intense gaze. Her mouth turned up at the corners a little, and I tucked that image in my heart. She was beautiful all the time, but when she smiled...wow. There were sparks, almost visible sparks, that danced back and forth between us. She charmed me utterly, bewitched me utterly, captivated and enchanted me, with her low, throaty voice, her sense of humor, her small acts of random kindness, the way she looked at me.

God, I had it bad.

"I'm glad you're here," she said again, her gaze pinning me to the spot. She licked her lips, tucked a stray strand of bright red hair behind her ear. She rocked back on her heels, gazed up at the brightly colored trees overhead. "I mean, we have a lot in common," she added helpfully.

I didn't mean to be obtuse, but I wasn't certain what she meant. My expression betrayed me.

"Well, for starters, we both have the Gay—with a capital G." She leaned in, winked at me. "Gay as a rainbow," she said, gesturing toward the sky. "Is that not a commonality between us, Miss Linden?" she said, affecting a posh British accent, which made me smile.

"Yes," I laughed. "But I don't think I ever would have called myself 'as gay as a rainbow'..."

"As gay as what, then, pray tell?" She sounded like a Shakespearean actress, and I chuckled at her joke, at the way she stayed, arms flung out on either side, eyebrow raised, teasing and awaiting my answer.

"I am as gay as..." I thought about this. I couldn't think of anything clever, so I settled on the first thing that came to mind: "A unicorn."

"Would you believe," she whispered conspiratorily, dropping her voice to an even sexier growl, "that the unicorns around here are not gay at all?"

I raised my eyebrows. "Surely you jest."

"I do not, madam!" She nodded curtly. "All of the unicorns in Wolf Town are as straight as, hmm—I don't know—George W. Bush."

"Wow. That's shockingly disappointing," I smiled. I snuck a little glance at her, and my cheeks warmed at the sight of her wide grin. I liked this. Us, laughing together on a brightly colored autumn walk. I cleared my throat, raised an eyebrow. "Okay, so what *else* do we have in common?"

"Um..." She cast about as she shoved her hands back into her pockets. "Aha! I know for a fact that we both like pumpkins!" she said, nodding toward a large pumpkin adorning the front stoop of a house we were passing.

I nodded, face schooled into seriousness. "I do like a good pumpkin," I told her, "but you're stereotyping!" I clicked my tongue and shook my head reproachfully. "You're using my witchiness for your own ends."

"I wouldn't dare," she smiled, and that was serious. She meant it.

"I mean, it *is* true," I said, trailing my hands along a conveniently placed picket fence. "I like pumpkins, and I like black cats. I love to wear purple and black. I have an apron that says 'Nothing says loving like something from the coven.'"

"That's so tacky!" Morgan groaned, laughing. "God, I *love* tacky things." I raised a brow skeptically, but she protested with a grin. "No, really! So, my cousin, Maddox, has this terrible sense of humor. I mean, terrible as in totally outrageous and ridiculous, not as in *bad*. Anyway," she said, spreading her hands, "he made the whole family matching sweatshirts last Christmas that say 'Never moon a werewolf.' I've worn mine so many times, it has holes in the cuffs."

"Oh, you're right — that is tacky, and I *love* it."

"Then you, madam, have most *excellent* taste." Morgan made a little bow, tossing her hair over her shoulder as she raised a single eyebrow and we continued walking along the street. "So," she told me, pausing and staring up, "this is a great place to start your all-expenses-paid Wolf Town historical tour." She smiled as she jerked a thumb toward a tall, steel-tipped fence. "This is Henry's place. He has a lake out back with a lake monster in it."

The house beyond the pointy fence was in disrepair: an old, broken-down mansion that may have once been painted burgundy, but the paint had now faded to a sickly shade between red and brown. The salt air of the ocean and the sea storms had beaten the house to a pulp, and the roof sagged dangerously to the right. I stood on my tiptoes and tried to see over the hedge but couldn't.

"Henry wouldn't mind if I showed you Ellie," said Morgan, smiling with mischief glinting in her green eyes. "I'm not gonna lie — she's kind of awesome."

"Um..." I said, which I think she thought meant "yes," because she was already opening the front gate and ushering me through.

"You will be amazed, shocked *and* awed," she assured me, putting her arm about my waist to steer me around a bend in the little path. My skin tingled where she touched me, and I hoped she didn't hear my quick intake of breath...

It was still light enough out to see the driveway make out the steps leading up to the old, unloved house. The porch was broad and rickety, but Morgan leapt up onto it in a heartbeat and used the large, antique-looking knocker (shaped like an ear of corn) once, twice.

A light flicked on in the hallway, and the door opened. A man shuffled out, peering with wide eyes into the gloom. He was probably in his late fifties, with thinning salt-and-pepper hair and bright eyes surrounded by laugh lines. He looked refined, like a college professor. He even wore a tweed jacket.

"Henry!" said Morgan, opening her arms. He ignored the offered hug and peered past her suspiciously.

"And who is this?" he asked. I tried smiling a little in the half-light.

"I'm Amy, sir," I said and extended my hand.

He didn't take it, only shook his head, patting his jacket pockets.

"I've brought her here to show off Ellie, if you don't mind," said Morgan, gesturing around the edge of the house.

"I've been having all sorts of damn trouble with her damn kids," said Henry, finding his glasses in his pants pocket, stepping off the porch, with Morgan following. I supposed this meant that we were going to meet Ellie. We trailed Henry's footsteps around the side of the house. "They keep getting out, Morgan," he muttered with a shake of his head. "It's becoming a real problem!"

There, behind the house, sprawled a wide, flat pond (decidedly not a lake) sporting several overly large lily pads and an ungodly amount of pond scum. In the dying light, the water looked almost flourescent green.

"Ellie!" shouted Henry, making me jump five feet. "C'mon, girl!" And then, he whistled, like he was calling for a particularly energetic puppy.

For a long moment, absolutely nothing happened.

And then the earth began to rumble.

And out of the water, she came.

First, the surface of the pond rippled outward from the center of the scummy body of water. Something broke that surface, like a log bobbing up from the bottom of the pond—but it wasn't a log. The object was shaped like an upside-down rowboat, and it was raised up on a thick neck. The rowboat-type thing was a head, I realized, and the neck was, well, a neck, and when Ellie towered upward, about twenty feet out of the water, and started coming toward us, blinking large, unreasonably cow-like eyes, I took a step backward and almost fell back, and *would* have fallen back if Morgan's strong arm wasn't there to catch me.

It was a lake monster. I mean, it was a…water-dinosaur-thing. A Loch Ness monster…

It was a Nessie.

But it wasn't a Nessie. It was an Ellie. And when Henry raised up his hand, the monster swam forward and bopped her gigantic nose into his palm as if she were nothing more than a gigantic (*really* gigantic) dog. Her head was about as tall as he was.

"This is Ellie," Henry said, peering

around her massive bulk to look at the water behind her. He wandered along the edge of the pond, whistling and calling. "C'mon, kids!"

"You can pet her if you want to," said Morgan with a wide smile, stepping forward to rub the giant's nose with the palm of her hand. "She's actually quite gentle."

I reached out my hand, too, tentatively, biting my lip hard. If Morgan hadn't been there, I don't think I would have chanced such bravado. As it was, I kind of quaked when Ellie turned, slowly, methodically, and then bopped her gigantic nose gently against *my* hand. Her skin felt like the sea turtle I'd touched at the aquarium once: smooth, leathery, and wet.

"She likes you!" said Morgan, grinning. But I wasn't convinced of myself, because Ellie chose that moment to (very slowly) draw her neck back and pull herself back down, by degrees, into the water. Her head disappeared underneath, leaving ripples on the surface of pond scum.

My hand dangled at my side and dripped onto the grass, the skin slightly slimy because there was algae on my fingers.

A lake monster…

I stared at the ripples disbelievingly.

But it had happened; Ellie was real.

"Thanks, Henry. It was so nice of you to show Ellie to Amy," said Morgan cheerfully as Henry turned to face the both of us.

"Listen—you tell your dad that I need help rounding up Ellie's kids," said Henry in a warning, distracted tone. Morgan saluted him, and we both began to walk back toward the gate.

"I promise I will," she called over her shoulder. Morgan ushered me through the fencing and out back into the night, shutting the iron gate behind us with a soft *clang*. I searched my jean pockets with my good hand for a tissue, and turning up empty-handed, I grimaced and wiped my palm on a the bark of the closest tree.

"*Wow*," I whispered, then stared at Morgan. The streetlights were bright enough to see her face, to see how happy she was—and to see that she was a little smug, too.

"Ulterior motive on that one," Morgan told me, one brow up, head tilted to the side as she held my gaze. "I knew she'd impress you."

"*Impress* might be the wrong word," I told her, burying my hands (that definitely needed washing) into my pockets, peering back over the top of the fence at Henry, who stalked along the edge of his pond, still whistling for water-dinosaur babies that were stubbornly refusing to materialize.

Then I stopped. "Wait," I said, drawing out the word thoughtfully. "You wanted to impress me?"

"Yeah," she admitted easily, shrugging her shoulders.

"Why?"

"Because," she said, drawing out her word, too, and stepping just a little bit closer. Her spicy scent flowed over me, and my heartbeat rose in a crescendo as I stared up at her. Morgan smiled her beautiful, crooked smile and cocked her head. "There's this new witch who came to town," she murmured, voice a low growl, "and I really like her."

My heart beat so hard, I thought it was going to pound itself out of my chest. "A new witch? Really?" I managed, finding it very difficult to breathe as I licked my lips. "Wait..." I said, blinking as I suddenly realized *exactly* what this meant. "You're not... I mean, you're not in a relationship?"

She looked surprised, shook her head. "No..." And then she chuckled a little. "No, I'm not—"

"It's just..." And I pointed to my ring finger, and she took her hands out of her pockets, stared down at them as if she'd never seen them before.

"Oh! Oh, that. It's my werewolf clan ring. See? It says 'MacRue' on it." She held up her hand for my inspection. I felt inordinately silly—and more than a little awkward—as I looked at it and remembered her father's ring, which was probably engraved with the same word.

"I like you, too," I said quietly, smiling

just a little. "So...now what do we do?"

"Huh," she grinned. And then, cocking her head, we both looked up at the first star coming out from behind the clouds in the dark purple sky. (That was a pretty auspicious sign, if you ask me.)

"Now...let's see what happens," she said in her low growl, and a thrill of possibility moved through the night, as bright as stars.

We shared a warm, expectant glance, and—unspeaking—we began to move down the sidewalk together. She reached across the space between us and took my hand in her warm palm. My heart skipped about a dozen beats as I breathed out a shaky, happy sigh.

Things were looking up—way up. As high as a heaven full of stars.

Chapter 6: The Fairy

"Hi, Mom!" I said, kicking my heels against the bedroom wall as I lay pillowed on my stomach on Aunt Bette's bed. "How are you?"

"Oh, Amy, honey, I'm wonderful! How are you? How's Wolf Town?"

Winnie sat next to me on the bed, primly reading some kind of see-through ghost book. I'd asked her what the book was about, and she quickly hid it from me. So I guessed it must be a "tawdry" novel from her era—a period romance that was actually...period. It likely involved literal bodice ripping, since the women in it likely wore actual bodices.

"Oh, things are, you know, great!" I said brightly. "But how's the coven? Do you have tonight's new moon ritual planned?" I'd been gone for less than a week, but one of our favorite shared activities was ritual planning, and I missed it.

"Well, I was thinking the ritual would be mostly meditation," she said, after some thought. I could hear the whistle of the tea kettle in the background. "But, seriously, honey. What's been happening? Give me details!"

"Well, Bette left the minute I arrived," I told her, with a shake of my head and a small smile. "I'm planning on reopening the café pretty soon. I just wanted to finish up painting it first."

"That's nice of you, dear," Mom said distractedly. I could hear the hot water being poured into a mug now. Then her voice turned coy: "And how are...*other* things?"

I sighed happily, acutely aware of the stupid smile spread over my face. Beside me, Winnie paused in her reading to roll her eyes. "Well...*other* things are...pretty great."

"Spill!" said my mother triumphantly. "I must know all!"

"I mean, I don't have a lot to tell you *yet*, but things are totally progressing toward...things," I told her, turning over onto my back. "But we can talk about that later." I cleared my throat, determined. "Mom...do you remember how you made that slightly ominous announcement about knowing the stories of Wolf Town?" I hadn't forgotten she'd said it, and it now made sense, considering the pond monsters, the vampire, the werewolves...

"Yeah?" she said, and I could almost *hear* her forehead wrinkling.

"It's kind of a strange place," I said quietly.

"Is it?"

I sighed and grinned, shaking my head. "Mom—"

"All right. The truth is...I lived there once. For a summer, to help your Aunt Bette with the café. Just like you're doing. I'll tell you about it, sometime. There's a reason you're there, sweetheart—"

"You don't say..." I smiled, tucked my thumb into my jeans' belt loop.

Ordinarily, I might have been a little put out over the fact that my mother had purposely failed to mention the small but *very* significant detail that she, too, had lived in Wolf Town.

But I wasn't put out. Because I liked it here. And, for whatever reason, I believed Mom when she said I was supposed to be here now.

"Sadly, I have to run," Mom began, which I knew was her way of suggesting that she didn't want me to try to pry anything else out of her. But what the heck was there to pry out? "We'll talk soon, sweetheart," she promised.

And then my mother suddenly ended the call.

"Huh," I muttered, staring down at the cell phone in my hand.

Weird.

It was a beautiful new moon evening, but the air had the scent of rain to it. As I stared at my aunt's bedroom ceiling, I sighed for a moment. I missed my mother. I missed the coven. I actually missed the sight of Tammie sprawled on the living room floor, trying to talk to her ancestors. I hadn't been homesick much since I'd arrived here—there had been too much to do, too much to take in—but in the almost-dark of the setting sun and no moon rising, I felt the prick of loneliness sting my heart.

I could have gone to the Ninth Order. I could have gone to the grocery store or the library. But I didn't. I pushed myself out of bed and grabbed my hoodie from the hook by the stove.

And I went out the back door of the café.

Behind the café and behind the main drag of the town, tall pine sentinels rose, stately and old. An entire ancient-looking forest bordered Wolf Town, which I thought to be quite intentional. Wolf Town seemed the kind of place where primordial forests were bound to thrive.

Now, witch ladies in autumn woods are a surefire recipe for mischief. *Knowing* this, I still didn't have any inclination to walk through town; it would be so nice, so enchanting, to take a quick starlit walk amongst the trees...

That's the stuff of magic, right? Of fairy tales?

I had never had any fear of the forest when I was a kid, and when I grew up, that feeling of safety beneath the trees remained obstinately with me. I was a witch: I knew the nature of, well, *nature*, like the back of my hand, could feel if something negative was close to me, could protect myself against it. There was nothing in the woods that could harm me if I regarded it with respect. I knew that fact deeply. I didn't fear the woods at night; I didn't fear the woods at all. So I shoved my hands deep into the pockets of my hoodie, just to warm them (it was chillier than I'd anticipated), and diverted off onto a wide path that entered the woods.

I'd been craving the time to explore these paths since I'd arrived. It was, admittedly, foolish to enter the woods for the first time at night, but under the trees, it felt warmer to me, like an embrace. As I walked along, I felt the encompassing gentleness of the trees around me, felt my energy mingle with theirs. I was safe, and I was held here, and, even though it was an October night, the favorite time of wandering spirits, I didn't feel any spirits close by. That was always a concern, in October. It was well known that, around the time of Samhain (otherwise known as Halloween), the door between the worlds thinned, the veil that separated the living and the dead became transparent, and ghosts or spirits could travel through easily and communicate with the other side. That's why there were so many séances around this time of year; we could communicate with the spirits just as readily as they could communicate with us.

So the basis of many horror or ghost stories actually stemmed from a very old and true fact: things that went bump in the night usually *bumped* most often around Halloween.

The path I'd found was wide and well kept, a packed-dirt path that wound its way through the stately trees. It was probably a bike or walking path for the inhabitants of Wolf Town. What was strange, however, is that unlike most bike paths, this one did not go forever in one direction, or loop back around to town (not that I'd seen yet). There was actually, before me now, an intersection of paths. A crossroads. I stared at that crossroads as I felt the hairs prick up along the back of my neck.

Witches had many superstitions, and one of them was this: crossroads, nearing All Hallow's Eve, were a place of mischief.

I stood for a long moment, the earlier security I'd felt in the forest beginning to wane. I was suddenly feeling…uncertain. There was something creeping just along the edges of my consciousness. I stood very still and *listened*, listened with my ears, my body, my heart.

The stars burned brightly overhead, and through the trees, I could see the streetlights of Wolf Town winking between the distant buildings.

But down the path and further into the woods, there bobbed…a different light.

I watched it curiously as it drifted closer.

It floated, this light, was carried by no creature, no man—it was only the light that came toward me, down the path, hovering in midair like a bumblebee or a bubble.

I had read of will-o'-the-wisps—many cultures have some mention of "witch lights" in their Spooky Literature collections—but I had never imagined that I might actually see one. And what else could this be? The sphere was about the size of my head, and it glowed with the light of a small sun. It bobbed along like a toy boat pulled by a very uncoordinated child, and it swayed this way and that but remained above the path.

As it drew closer to me, I stepped back a little. I thought it might move through me or into me, but it didn't, instead hovering about two feet away from me as it drew to a slow standstill.

It was just a sphere of light, nothing more, and it was hardly ominous-looking, but I had never encountered anything like it before. I wasn't fully educated yet in the weirdness of Wolf Town, and the will-o'-the-wisp could turn out to be a not-so-nice creature... Still, it didn't *feel* like a dark entity to me.

The sphere of light suddenly darted a little to the left, and a little to the right. Then it moved back two feet and remained, hovering.

It repeated that odd little dance move again: a little to the left, a little to the right—back again.

Was it...beckoning me to follow?

Hmm. Didn't every fairy tale or myth or piece of folklore that involved these things end up with someone being lured to their death by drowning in a bottomless bog? Not that there were all that many *bogs* populating New England, but caution forced me to wonder...

I shook my head—I wasn't keen on idea of following it—and turned to go, but it darted in front of me, still twinkling.

Again, it edged a bit away, hovered and waited.

I reached out my hand, cocked my head, and it came to me, floating above the palm of my hand.

"What do you want?" I asked, as clearly and loudly as I could. The little sphere quivered and shook, and then it shook again, as if it was a head and was saying *no*.

How could a sphere of light say *no*?

This could not possibly get any stranger.

After a full minute of frowning and sighing and deep, soul-searching consideration...I decided to follow the thing. I mean, it was a floaty ball of light—the stuff of fairy tales and ghost stories! My curiosity, admittedly, got the best of me.

But I wasn't stupid. I kept my ears open and my eyes peeled and kept casting about, waiting for a dragon to leap out from between the trees, or for a headless horseman to come galloping in my direction, or for some other supernatural threat that this will-o'-the-wisp wanted to guide me toward, meant to usher in my untimely demise.

We paused for a moment, the orb floating in front of me as if to get its bearings; then it turned to the right, leaving the path. I remained exactly where I was, hands deep in my pockets, watching it as it drifted down toward a valley in the woods.

It stopped, floating, waiting for me.

I drew in a deep breath. And against my better judgment, I followed it off the path.

The wind was cold against my neck. The fluttering of bats along the edges of the treeline was almost like music. I paused, feeling the cool touch of the air along my skin, feeling the touch of something I couldn't see. I closed my eyes for a long moment, drawing energy into me from the woods to form a shield of white light around myself. And then I opened my eyes.

There was a sound, like bells, a crystalline chiming that shone in the air, surrounding me. I opened my mouth and shut it, turning as I stood in the center of that little dip in the woods. I could see nothing, but as I turned, I heard it again and again, heard it come nearer to me from over the hill.

The orb arced toward the source of the chiming. Finally, it paused, simply floating. I passed the orb, climbing the hill and marching up and over the lip of the bluff.

Through the woods moved tall horses, horses I could see even in the darkness, because their saddles and bridles, their hooves and eyes, their manes and tails, glowed with an unearthly light. Tiny embroidered bells of silver chimed along their bridles as they moved, as they tossed their great heads and pawed the earth with massive hooves. As impressive, majestic and fantastical as the horses were, however, they were greatly outshone by their riders.

They were beautiful beyond description; their skin flickered, changing like fire, and their eyes blazed brighter than a star. They wore fine silks, shimmering fabrics that were every color and no color, changing in the light of their celestial mounts. Their faces were long and pointed, with extra wide eyes that glowed brightly.

And streaming from their shoulders and over the backs of their horses, almost long enough to graze the dark earth, lay luminescent, bright-colored wings.

Fairies.

I knew without a shadow of a doubt that these were fairies. I had never seen any sight so beautiful in all of my life.

The horse in the lead was taller than the others, the woman (I assumed it was a woman—the only thing that differentiated her from her companions was the outward curve of her chest) shone brighter, a circlet of flashing blue over her hair and the skin of her brow. The others deferred to her as she stood up in her stirrups, sniffing the wind with a distinctly royal nose. A...queen? Was this a fairy court?

I stood on the edge of the bluff as the leader turned—turned and, without a doubt, saw me. Her eyes narrowed. She pointed one long-nailed finger that did not waver. The others turned and stared at me, too.

The little glowing orb darted down the hill and danced above the leader's hand. She plucked it out of the air, and it grew smaller, weaker, until it was about the size of a grape. Then she tossed the orb of light into her mouth and swallowed it, licking her lips with a long blue tongue.

I backed up one step, and then another. She had not taken her eyes from me.

I thought about the story of Tam Lin, and I thought about the old world legends of wicked fairies...and the beauty of this vision before me began to pale a little bit.

Okay, so most people think of fairies as adorable, darling creatures, like Tinkerbell in *Peter Pan*. But if you explore the ancient stories? Fairies are pretty damn awful. They kidnap people all the time, for starters. A lot of the superstitions we use today, like horseshoes above doorways, come from the fact that iron could keep evil fairies out, could prevent them from hurting you and yours. People in Europe believed without a shadow of a doubt that fairies were harmful, evil beings.

And here I was, staring at an entire court of them.

I could never make it to the town if I ran now. I could never outrun these huge, sleek horses with muscles that rippled like *satin* beneath their fur. I swallowed, and, softly, gently, I imagined a sphere of white light encompassing me again, seeing it glow brighter in my mind's eye. Not that this shield would effectively deter fairy hunters from tracking me through the woods and subsequently eating me up, like some updated version of "Little Red Riding Hood." But it made me feel *slightly* more confident.

Slightly…

The leader dismounted from her beast effortlessly, striding toward me. She towered two feet above me, moved across the forest floor as if it were water and she was gliding over its surface. The earth almost seemed to undulate beneath her feet, the draping, luminous wings trailing along behind her glowing in the dark.

I stared up at her, my chin pointing up to the sky, as I gazed into her fathomless black eyes.

"Can you see us?" she whispered, drawing close. The fabric of her cape shimmered, and her words were so soft, I had to strain to hear her, to understand her. I shook my head, pressed my hands together, my nails digging into my palms as if the sharpness of the sensation could ground me, make me focus. Maybe it did. She'd stopped flickering in my line of sight, at least. She no longer looked liked a mirage.

She was very beautiful. In the creepy kind of way that a perfect, well-made doll is beautiful.

"I can see you," I replied. I wasn't sure if I should bow or curtsy, so I just stood there and nodded, half-bent over at the waist.

She cocked her head, did not respond, and instead began to circle me, her posture shark-like, predatory.

"You have the scent of wolf on you," she said, darting close, sniffing my shoulder. She smelled of bonfires and burning. She wrinkled her long pale nose, backed away. "Werewolf."

I didn't answer her, only straightened and stood my ground, watching her carefully.

"Wolf...wolf..." came the soft chanting from the others. They whispered it amongst themselves, and the horses shifted, bells tinkling, nervous.

"You might be just what we need," said the fairy woman then, cocking her head the other way. She had not blinked this entire time. "Give me your hand, human."

I shook my head, backed away, but then I was standing stock still, as if cement had been poured into my veins and instantly hardened.

I couldn't move.

She snatched my fingers up, dropped something cool into them, and stalked back to the assembled horses and riders. When she mounted, her beast reared up, thrashing his great forelegs into the night, eliciting sparks from the thin air.

And then they turned, all of them, and, as one, moved off into the darkness of the woods, their mounts gallopping until horses and riders were gobbled up by the cold October night.

In my hand was an envelope the color of moonlight. "Allen MacRue" was written on it in a looping, cursive hand.

A letter from a fairy queen to a werewolf patriarch.

And I, the messenger witch.

Chapter 7: The Family

"That's strange," said Winnie, with minimal helpfulness.

I sighed, took a very deep, cleansing breath, and tried again. "So, what you're telling me—and I'm repeating this just so that I absolutely, positively have this right—is that there *are* nice fairies and mischievous fairies in the vicinity of Wolf Town, but there is *no* impressive fairy-court-type fairies in or around Wolf Town at *all,* that you know of."

Winnie thought about this for a very long moment, wrinkling her nose. She crossed her legs the other way, hanging suspended in the air as if she were sitting on an invisible beanbag chair. "That is correct," she answered me, tilting her head to the side. "But if you like," she suggested, "I can speak to the other ghosts. I, personally, have never heard of a fairy court located anywhere near Wolf Town." She glanced at the letter with a suspicious frown, the words *Allen MacRue* penned across the cream-colored envelope in ornate, glimmering silver paint. Winnie raised a single eyebrow. "She said to deliver it to Allen?"

"Yes." I turned the envelope over again, staring at the complex, beveled seal on the back. The wax was silver and glittery, and the complex knotwork that had been pressed into the seal seemed to move and shift in front of my eyes as if the knotwork were, in fact, a pair of waxy snakes writhing on the parchment.

"Do you know where the MacRue house is?" asked Winnie, pointing out the window toward the hill at the other end of town. "It's right on the hilltop. It's actually very easy to get to. You could walk there. Are you going to deliver it, like she asked?"

I shuddered. I loved a good, cool night walk, but I figured it'd be a long time before I ventured out on a voluntary one again. They had been beautiful, those fairies, but there had been something extremely...*uncaring* about them. As if they had found me utterly beneath them.

So I was wondering now if a night jaunt was a wise—or safe—idea.

"Don't you think," said Winnie reasonably, "that it's best to get this over with?"

I didn't have to deliver the letter. There was no law in the universe that stated a random fairy horde could order me to do anything they damn well pleased.

But at the same time...did I *want* to piss them off?

I sighed for a very long time before I made up my mind.

"Good luck," Winnie told me as I shut the café door behind me.

I compromised. Yes, perhaps the MacRue house was within walking distance. But I didn't want to chance another encounter with, well, *anything*. I unlocked the door to my Subaru, revved the engine, and turned my car's nose toward the distant hilltop.

There were candles burning in the windows of every house I passed, with orange and purple lights strung along the porch railings. Jack-o-lanterns grinned at me from front steps, and tattered sheets danced in the trees as ghosts. The wind blew puffs of leaves ahead of the car in a steady, colorful procession as I motored up the road in the hillside, winding toward the MacRue clan house.

Winnie had said I couldn't miss the MacRue mansion when I approached it—and she was right. I passed by a Halloween tableau, complete with bales of hay, about twenty jack-o-lanterns, and handmade scarecrows, all gathered around a beautifully painted wooden sign staked into the ground reading *MacRue*. A hall of gigantic oak trees stretched down the remaining portion of the road that had somehow turned into a driveway when I wasn't looking. And there, at the foot of the driveway, was the mansion.

The house was bigger than an old Catholic school, with just as many wings. It didn't necessarily look New England-y. More like a castle in Europe. The outer structure of the mansion was built entirely of stone; it stood ancient-looking and imposing, sprawling across the grounds. And there was a candle burning in every one of the dozens of front windows, flickering brightly.

The tableau of hay bales and jack-o-lanterns had been impressive enough, but the Halloween decorations adorning the house itself would have made Martha Stewart herself envious.

There were orange lights strung around the edges of the roof, looping around each window, and the front columns were twined with purple lights. Bales and bales of hay, along with pumpkins and gourds and bunches of cornstalks, covered the porch, all of the pumpkins lit and elaborately carved. There were witch silhouettes in the windows, and the door had a gigantic illuminated sign made out of orange lights: *BEWARE*.

Honestly, I had never seen a house surpass my mother's obsessive Halloween decorating before. Until now.

I got out of my car and paused for a long moment, fingers on the handle of the car door, my other hand clutching the cream-colored envelope. Allen MacRue. The guy in the grocery store. I bit my lip. I'd gotten a bad feeling from him...but he was Morgan's father, so maybe my instincts were a little off. Wolf Town had set me a little off-kilter, after all.

Still, as I approached the porch, a small but persistent thought wheedled at me: I really hoped Allen MacRue wasn't home. I could just shove the letter through the mail slot and be on my merry way.

The porch had those motion-sensor Halloween decorations that cackle and scream *boo* at you if you're unfortunate enough to walk in front of them. There were several mannequin zombies sprawled across the hay bales, and one vampire dressed to look like an exact imitation of the Dracula from the old black-and-white movie. He happened to cackle like the Count from Sesame Street, adding his animatronic voice to the moaning zombies as I sighed and—amidst the cacaphony—knocked on the front door.

It was a very light knock, but soon enough I heard footsteps. I took a deep breath, tossed my hair back, squared my shoulders, and glanced up into Allen MacRue's face as he opened the door.

"Amy!" he said, with a bright smile that flickered a little and never reached his eyes. I saw that flicker instantly, even though he tried to hide it by deepening his wide smile. Behind him, further back into the house, I could hear many voices and laughter inside. He kept the door purposefully narrowed as he cleared his throat and said formally, "What brings you to this neck of the woods?"

"Um," I said articulately, and gripped the letter a little harder. I opened and closed my mouth, realizing I hadn't thought this through. How *exactly* was I going to explain this to him? I cleared my throat, tried to simplify what had just happened to me, and settled on, "Did you know that there are fairies in the Wolf Town woods?"

He didn't even skip a beat. "Of course there are," he said, grinning indulgently. I didn't like that expression on his face. It was condescending. "They're quite lovely. They dance in circles, steal things, sometimes eat cats... They're mischievous but don't cause any real harm."

I bit my tongue over the cat comment (he *was* a werewolf, after all), and kept going, through gritted teeth. "No... I mean, I don't mean *those* fairies. That's nice that they're there, but I'm talking about..." I trailed off, trying to think about how to describe the beings I'd encountered in the woods. "*Larger* fairies?" I tried, holding up my hand about a foot or so over my own head to indicate height. "Kind of like a fairy court? On horses? Really big and a little scary, like a fantasy movie gone creepy?"

He watched me with flickering eyes that narrowed as I spoke. He was pinning me in a gaze that was so hungry, so intense, it allowed me to see the wolf sleeping within him. It felt predatory, the way he held me to the spot with those unblinking, slitted eyes.

He cleared his throat then, and leaned forward. "What *about* those fairies?" he growled, voice hardly above a whisper.

I swallowed. "I went for a walk in the woods tonight," I said with a frown. "And I...sort of ran into this orb, at a crossroads..."

He didn't even listen. He'd seen the envelope in my hands, and upon sighting it, he'd paled further. Now he reached out and snatched the envelope from my grasp.

I stood, speechless, as he began to close the door. "It was lovely seeing you again, Amy..." he mumbled insincerely, as the door nearly slammed in my face.

But then:

"Amy, is that you?" came a laughing voice, and the door was wrenched open, and Morgan stood there, her fantastic mane of hair floating around her face like flames. Her eyes, too, seemed to burn as she took me in.

Allen's expression darkened with displeasure, but he forced a smile as Morgan stepped forward and drew me toward her in a tight embrace. "I wasn't expecting you!" She smiled, and then hugged me tighter still. She smelled like woodsmoke and leaves, and though my night had been very strange (and things had just gotten a hell of a lot stranger), I held onto her, wrapping my arms around her back. "It's so good to see you..." she growled into my ear, and I shivered at the sound of her voice, at the heat of her breath against my skin.

"Amy's here?!" came a high-pitched squeal, and then a kid ran around the corner and right into Morgan, who stepped out of hugging me, caught the girl and tickled her stomach without skipping a beat. The girl had the same long red hair and bright green eyes as Morgan, and when she looked up at me, I could see the same mischievous tilt in her nose.

"Amy, this is my niece, Moira," said Morgan, poking the girl in the stomach again. "Moira, say hello to Amy, you little beastie."

"Hello, Amy!" she told me obediently before she literally bounced out of Morgan's grasp and tore off back down the hallway, running right past her grandfather. "Grandpa, Grandpa, *Grandpa*, they're heeeere!"

Allen sighed and smiled.

A grinning man poked his head out of the same room Moira had come from. "Is this Amy?" He, too, had that shock of red hair that Morgan and Moira sported, but his was close-cropped. He came forward, smiling widely — baring his collection of pointy teeth — and extended a hand. "I'm Maddox," he told me, with a toss of his head, green eyes flashing. "It's lovely to meet you. We've heard so much about you!"

"Maddox is my cousin. We, uh...have a big family," explained Morgan, running a long-fingered hand through her hair, sending the red locks out in all directions.

Behind her, Allen MacRue was turning quietly away, tucking the letter into his pants pocket, but Morgan glanced over her shoulder, spotted him trying to leave and practically pounced on him, hooking an arm through his.

"Dad, this is Amy," she told him, as he was turned toward me, and I stood there, uncertain. I mean, I'd met him before. I'd just delivered him a letter that he hadn't seemed too happy about receiving. This was more awkwardness than I was prepared to deal with after my harrowing run-in with a fairy queen.

But Allen breezed past all that, hiding his annoyance behind an impressively convincing smile. "Welcome to our home, Amy," he said, practically purring as he inclined his head toward me. "And welcome to Wolf Town. I'm Allen MacRue!" he said, with the sort of flourish that a bad (or an ironic) actor makes, and then he took a step forward and hugged me—which startled me so much that I stiffened against him.

It was a quick embrace, and when it was over, he held me out at arm's length, hands on my shoulders, scrutinizing my face as if he'd never seen me before, or as if he was memorizing my features. I lifted a brow.

"It's good to have you here," he said;

then, with a slow nod of his head and wide eyes, he cleared his throat. "We were just going to order pizza."

Morgan ushered us into a side room that looked and felt exactly like a Victorian parlor. There were loveseats that should have been in a museum (and never, ever sat on), floral wallpaper, ornate mahogany china cabinets and tall, round tables with sculpted legs. I glanced around, a little awed as I tried to take everything in, but then Moira dashed into the room and literally ran into me, a small foot kicking out against my shin as she tried to make herself stop.

"Amy, Amy, Amy!" she said, bouncing up and down. "Do you want to see what I can do?"

"Sure!" I said, just as Morgan said, "Don't!" And then Moira was doing a handstand and walking on her hands beside me. Except she was only able to take one step before she toppled over and fell into one of the loveseats, sprawling against the carved leg with an audible *thunk* that would probably have made any normal kid black out. But not Moira. She bounced back up and started to throw herself forward again onto her hands—but Morgan caught her, shaking her head with a stern look.

"Not in the house, sweetie," she sighed, and Moira shrugged, running back out of the room on some urgent mission.

"We raise them like wolves around here," said Maddox apologetically, even as he grinned at his cousin. Morgan groaned and rolled her gorgeous green eyes.

"Yeah, well," she said, mouth twitching with a smile. "Even wolves can learn manners."

A few more people began to drift into the room. Most were redheads, though there were a few brunettes in the mix. They were all about a head or so taller than me; some were young, but most of them were probably between their thirties to fifties, lovely men and women, handsome and beautiful in turns. They looked positively otherworldly.

"This is most of the MacRue clan," said Allen, waving his hand.

Several of the clan murmured greetings to me, but it was a little unnerving, having so many people stare—judging me, I knew. They were wondering if I was good enough for their Morgan.

"Family reunion?" I murmured to Morgan, who glanced at me with a shrug as she folded her arms in front of her.

"They're here for Halloween. It's a...big deal in Wolf Town," she said in a low, growling voice, even as she smiled at me—instantly turning my knees to jelly. For that smile, I'd put up with a million people judging me. A billion...

"So, you're a witch?" Maddox asked then,

once more people had rambled in and settled onto the aforementioned loveseats. With all of the people gathered together in the room, you could certainly tell that they were related. And Morgan had a *very* large family.

I took a deep breath. Morgan had probably told them I was a witch. It still unnerved me a little that they knew this about me, before they'd ever met me.

"Yes," I told them with a small smile. I straightened my back, standing a little taller. "I come from a long line of witches—the Linden witches."

"I've heard of your mother," said Allen then, pouring himself a glass of brandy from an ornate sidetable. He turned to me with an unreadable, shrewd gaze as he sniffed his glass and said mildly, "She's supposed to be quite good."

"Thank you," I managed. How did this man know of my mother? Had they crossed paths when Mom lived in Wolf Town?

"So, Amethyst is watching the café for Bette while she enjoys a vacation," Morgan announced to her gathered relatives.

"Really?" asked Allen sharply.

My hackles were rising, and I opened my mouth to respond when the doorbell rang. It sounded like cathedral chimes, echoing through the halls.

"Pizza!" Moira screamed, and she lunged

herself off of the loveseat to tear around the corner.

Allen brushed past me on his way out to the hallway.

There was something about that man that I didn't like. He gave me such a foreboding feeling. How could he possibly be related to Morgan, whose presence made me feel so excited and light?

"Pizza, pizza, pizza!" Moira chanted from the other room. Then she came flying back into the parlor with a huge slice in her hands.

So, one of the strangest things you can ever see, I firmly believe, is a werewolf clan tearing into ten boxes of pizza. "Did you get the anchovy one?" "Share with your brother!" "I hate onions!" (I thought onions were poisonous to dogs, but I supposed werewolves must be different.) "There's not enough cheese on this!" There was an initial scrabble in the long dining hall, and then Morgan and I helped ourselves to the remaining pieces.

"What kind of magic can you do?" asked a lanky young man, his red hair bunched back into a ponytail. "I'm Brandon, by the way," he said, grinning over his pizza sandwich. "Morgan's nephew."

I waved my slice of pizza in the air; I sat perched on the edge of one of the antique loveseats. "Just…glamours and spells and run-of-the-mill, New Agey stuff…" I trailed off.

"You know, the usual witchcrafts."

"Can you do weather magic? The last witch in Wolf Town could, like, make it rain and stuff," said Moira, bouncing up and down on the loveseat next to me, almost causing the extremely expensive china plate on my lap to fall to the floor. I steadied it, smiling at her.

"I don't think I've ever made it rain, but, to be fair, I've never tried."

"What about broomstick riding?" asked Maddox.

This was starting to feel like an interrogation. "Um..." I looked around at the assembled werewolves. "I'm a *witch*," I said carefully.

"We know. I'm asking if you can ride a broomstick," said Maddox. "The last witch who lived here could."

"What? I'm not that kind of witch..." I told them, perplexed. Honestly, I'd had to deal with this question before—many, many times before, actually. People think they're funny with the broomstick bit, think it's original, not knowing that every witch has probably been asked that particular question ten million times. But I'd never been asked it with any sort of seriousness before. And Maddox was being utterly serious. I cleared my throat. "I'm sorry," I told him, shaking my head, "but when I say *witch*, I mean I'm a Pagan, a Goddess-worshipping ritualist with a tendancy toward composting and tarot cards." I tried a smile. "What do *you* guys mean when you say *witch*?"

They all exchanged a meaningful glance. I tried—and somewhat failed—to keep smiling.

"Well," said Maddox slowly, "I suppose like the last one. She rode a broomstick and wore a black hat quite a bit. She liked to conjure imps."

I put my face in my hands as I took a deep breath.

"Great. So, like a typical Halloween cartoon witch. A storybook witch," I muttered. Then I looked up. "That's...actually a real thing?"

"Is being a Pagan, Goddess-worshipping whatever a real thing?" asked Moira. The child wasn't being snide; she was perfectly sincere.

"Yes," I told her, without question.

"Tabitha admitted that she gravitated towards the cliché side of witchcraft," said Maddox smoothly. "You just gravitate towards the, well, more mundane side. Correct?"

I absolutely, positively, could not tell if he meant that as a compliment, an insult, neither, or both.

I mean, it was now an established fact that there were werewolves and fairies and vampires in Wolf Town. It shouldn't have been so surprising to me that there were (supposedly) people who could ride brooms and conjure imps out of thin air. I think a lot of witches *wish* we could do such things…but it had always seemed, well, make-believe.

Not…*real.*

With my head reeling, I dropped the remainder of my pizza slice back onto my plate.

Morgan leaned closer to me then. She was sitting on the other side of me, her thigh brushing up against mine. She was keeping me grounded. The spicy scent of her brought me back to reality, and when she gently bumped her shoulder against me, I turned to her with a soft smile.

"Penny for your thoughts?" she asked quietly, her low voice a delicious growl that made me shiver a little, even as I took a deep breath and tried to steady myself.

Even though I currently found myself in a very unexpected circumstance (a werewolf pizza party is pretty unexpected, if you ask me), there was a connection between us, a gravity connecting us.

I turned to her like a plant turns toward the sun.

"Has anyone told you about the Hallow's Eve Fair?" said Morgan gently.

I shook my head, and, in front of her entire family, she put her arm firmly about my shoulder, drawing me closer and caving my body against her own. The protective arm and her bodily stance communicated, "Stop poking her with questions."

"So, Dad puts on a carnival in town every year," said Morgan quietly, searching my eyes with her own bright green ones. "It's called the Hallow's Eve Fair. It's...wonderful. Magical," said Morgan, her head tilted to the side as she smiled and held my gaze. "I think you'll love it, Amy."

"There's a gigantic Ferris wheel! And it's *orange* like a *pumpkin*," said Moira, jabbing my arm from the side. "And there are games! And a dance! It's a masquerade ball!" She ran off toward the dining room.

"Moira's had a lot of sugar today," said Morgan thoughtfully. "Perhaps too much."

"Halloween is our favorite time here in Wolf Town. We are always ourselves, but—on Halloween—well...it's a celebration of our differences," said Allen then, sitting back in his chair comfortably, holding my gaze. "We pride ourselves on celebrating differences in Wolf Town..."

Moira darted back into the parlor and dashed around the loveseat. She placed a pumpkin-shaped cookie into my lap before tearing back toward the dining room again, like a sugar-coated pixie hell bent on pizza consumption.

As Morgan traced a finger over my shoulder, and as I raised the cookie to my mouth, the lull and murmur of the wolves around us calmed me. Even as Allen continued to watch me with a small frown.

The cookie tasted like autumn.

"Forgive my family," said Morgan on the porch, after the awesome-but-still-exceedingly-awkward dinner came to an end. "They can be a little...wolfish sometimes," she said, with a small chuckle and a sideways smile.

We were out standing on the gravel drive in front of the brightly lit mansion. I could head faint voices and laughter emanating from within, but out here, it was pretty quiet. And a little cold. Overhead, there were a million stars, and beneath them all, there was Morgan and me.

She stood there, rocking back on her heels, her hands stuck deep into her jeans pockets as her body curved toward me.

I took a deep breath. I had to know the truth.

"Are there really fairy tale witches in existence, Morgan?" I asked her, searching her face. In truth, the very idea of it was half-exciting. But it was also half-really weird to think that all of the stereotypes and cliches I'd fought against my whole life could possibly be true. The idea of werewolves and vampires and pond monsters existing was awesome. But the existence of a cackling, bubbling cauldron-stirring witch was going to affect me personally.

I waited, holding my breath. And when Morgan nodded, I sighed.

"But there aren't any more witches in Wolf Town these days," she said hastily. "Tabitha was one of the last ones—"

I pinched the bridge of my nose. The witch's name had been Tabitha. Of course. Oh, God, the cliché of it all.

"Do you want me to walk you home?" she asked then. I glanced up at her, gazing into her bright, flickering eyes, but then I took a deep breath, remembering, and jerked my thumb toward my car.

"I drove here," I said, rubbing my shoulders in the chill autumn wind.

"Are you all right?" she asked, her voice a low, comforting growl. "You seem a little frazzled."

"Yeah," I lied, rubbing my arms in the chill dark. "I'm okay."

I didn't know how to tell her that her father gave me bad vibes. I didn't know how to bring up the fact that fairies had found me in the woods, had given a mysterious letter to me to be delivered to her dad.

I was in over my head in Wolf Town. Already. And I knew it.

Morgan brought me back to reality, helped me get out of my head. She leaned forward, touched my upper arm with warm fingers, wrapping her arm around my shoulders and drawing me close. She smelled so good, so cinnamon-y and warm and inviting as she pulled me toward her and held me tightly for a long moment, her chin propped on top of my head.

I was almost relaxed against her until she said, "My dad..." She rumbled the words against me with a sigh. "He's sort of the patriarch of the town. It was really important to me that you met him, Amy. I'm glad you did."

I nodded. I wasn't sure I exactly agreed that my meeting him was necessary, but I nodded, anyway. And then, because I'd been wondering, I asked quietly, "And your mom?"

Morgan shook her head, stepped back from me, though she still held me around the shoulders with both arms as she searched my gaze. "My mother died when I was a kid," she said quietly. "I never knew her."

I swallowed and bit my lip. I couldn't imagine that. True, I had grown up without a dad. Mom and my father hadn't stayed together, had, in fact, split up when I was too little to remember what having two parents had been like. He didn't want much to do with me. I had been raised by a mother's influence alone, and I couldn't envision what it might have been like to have no mother at all. A great lump of homesickness flooded me for a moment, even as Morgan's arms tightened around me, and I felt the warmth of her, right there, solid and real.

Despite everything that had happened this evening, I took a deep breath. "I'm glad I came tonight," I said, which *was* the truth. I was glad that I'd seen her, glad that I was right here, right now. I took her hand, threaded her fingers through mine.

It was a bright night, and the gravel driveway shone with the light from the porch of the mansion, a golden glow that seemed to fill the chill air with honeyed warmth. When I turned toward Morgan, her red hair, fanning over her shoulders in crimson waves, seemed to glow in that golden light, flickering like fire.

I knew, more than anything, at that moment that I had to kiss her.

I was a little tentative when I moved forward, when I wrapped an uncertain arm around her waist, another around her shoulders. I stood up on tiptoe and bent my head back, and as she leaned toward me, as she sighed out and gripped my hips with sure hands, I kissed her gently on the mouth, opening my lips to hers, surprised and delighted by how absolutely soft they were, how they tasted like pomegranates (her favorite, often-applied lip balm), and how she was so warm, she made me melt against her.

Morgan's fingers dug into my hips gently, her hands resting against my waist, their reassuring presence warm and unwavering as she held me firmly. She kissed me back, opening her mouth to me, tasting me and drinking me in.

I wanted to see her kissing me, wanted to see how close we were, so even though it felt strange, I opened my eyes wide, saw her own eyes closed, and so near to mine, her glittering eye shadow flashing in the porch light.

My heart was beating so loudly within me that we seemed to follow a rhythm all our own as we stood together, linked and embracing and kissing one another fiercely.

She broke away, smiling down at me, her eyes sly as she began to chuckle. Then we laughed a little — that awkward moment after the kiss, when I wondered if I should make a joke, or if I should kiss her again, and everything was silly and golden, and she looked so happy.

She put her fingers on my shoulder, slid them up to the curve at the base of my head, gently turning in my hair. "That was lovely," she said, then leaned a little closer. "*You* are lovely."

I didn't know what to say. No one had ever told me I was lovely before. I could feel the blush creeping over my skin and flushing my face, and I breathed out, suddenly aware of how close she was, how warm she was, how she held me like she might never let go. It felt right; all of this felt so right, and when she lowered her head to kiss me again, I savored the moment, savored the starshine and the way her long red hair brushed over my forehead as she bent over me, and the way that she reminded me of apple cider—warm and hot and spicy.

Despite potentially evil fairies and that shady Allen MacRue...my terrible night had turned out to be not such a terrible night after all.

In fact, it was positively *magical*.

Chapter 8: The Mermaid

So...the Witch Way Café had been open for approximately—I checked my watch—four hours, and thus far?

Not a single customer.

"Don't worry," Winnie assured me as I stood, hands on my hips, and stared out the open front door at the people walking on the sidewalk, striding right past. "Your aunt never had that many customers to begin with," she said, stretching overhead as she floated in a seated position next to me. She put her see-through chin in her see-through hands and cast me a sidelong glance.

"Well, I *am* worried," I told her with an agitated sigh. "I mean, *no* customers? I've put up a sign that says 'We're back in business!' and I've lit up the *open* sign, and—let's be honest—it's not as if there are all that many places to *eat* in Wolf Town."

"You're forgetting," said Winnie with raised eyebrows, "that a lot of these residents don't exactly...um...*eat* what's on your aunt's menu."

I paused and bit my lip, letting her words sink in. "Okay, that's a little creepy," I told her with a small smile. But, joking aside, I was worried that my aunt would come back from her vacation all happy and rested, and go to check the cash register…and realize that her niece had netted her a big, fat, whopping zero.

I supposed it was time to do a little magic.

I sighed again, turned and strode back to the counter. I stood behind it, straightened my shoulders, and stretched my arms overhead, taking a deep breath. And then I closed my eyes.

Used to my witchy shenanigans by this point, Winnie didn't even remark.

I imagined:

All of the folks of Wolf Town coming into the cafe — every chair and booth in the café filled, coffee brewing and bubbling, the teapot singing, me flipping pancakes and omelettes over the back stove. Everyone who wandered through Wolf Town stopping at the café, ordering a plate of bacon or flapjacks, drinking the magical coffee and filling my aunt's cash register with well-folded and creased cash.

I imagined this for as long as I could hold the image, my heart warming at the vision. And then I opened my eyes, took another deep breath. I'd set the intention for the space. Now I just had to believe it utterly and keep doing what I was doing.

"So mote it be," I whispered.

A knock at the shop door shattered the silence. An apologetic Burt Halek peered through the glass.

"So sorry to trouble you again, Amy," he said, out of breath. He huffed in and out as he stood in the doorway, leaning on the doorjamb like it was the only thing keeping him upright. "I wanted to let you know that the water is going to have to be turned off again—"

"Again! Wow..." I faltered, but nodded encouragingly to him. "Please don't worry about it—it's all right, Burt. You can turn it off right away."

"Wish us luck, Amy? This is getting ridiculous. I don't really know what to do, what keeps blocking it... It almost seems hopeless," he sighed, and turned to go.

I remembered what Winnie and Morgan had said about lake monsters—and the likelihood of Ellie's dubious offspring clogging the pipes.

"Wait, Burt!" I called, grabbing my hoodie from the peg by the door. It read "Salem Witch," which was only half true, but it was very warm. "Maybe I can help?" I offered. I felt, in my bones, that I needed to offer him assistance.

Burt didn't refuse me, which demonstrated just how desperate he really was. I wasn't a plumber, after all.

He nodded, gestured for me to follow him, and after I switched off the *open* sign on the café window, we trotted off down the street, the October sun honeying the noon hour.

The water pipes for the entire town were connected beneath the old Gymbon plant, a factory that Burt had informed me once made shoes. Now it was abandoned — really one of the only places in Wolf Town that wasn't well kept or loved, it seemed. The large brick building squatted on the far edge of town, overgrown with trees, shrubs and sumac, the windows smashed — probably by rowdy teenagers. Burt let us in through the chainlink fence recently erected around the property, unlatching the big lock affixed to the gate.

"Originally, we thought it might have been one of Ellie's get that kept messing up the pipes," he told me, as he swung the gate closed behind us and we walked up to the plant entrance. "But we've found no trace of any of them, and Ellie hasn't been reproducing this past month. Henry said he took away all of her eggs." He sighed and cast his eyes heavenward. "How a lake monster manages to reproduce without a sire helping the equation... Well. I guess there are weirder things in Wolf Town."

I laughed, then sobered as I realized that

he hadn't meant his words to be funny.

"Hey—do you hear that?" I asked suddenly.

Singing. A woman's voice, high and sweet. I couldn't make out any of the words...

Burt and I exchanged a glance and then ventured into the abandoned factory.

Since most of the windows had been broken, shattered glass littered the ground, sparkling and reflecting the sky peeking through the holes in the faraway roof. There were exposed beams curving down to meet us from overhead, and the eerie sound of a chain clinking against the sheet metal wall made the hair on the back of my neck stand to attention. We startled a small flock of pigeons roosting in the rafters, which flew from one end of the room to the other. A few disturbed white feathers drifted down at our feet.

My skin pricked again, and I put a hand on Burt's arm. He paused, took a flashlight out of his coat pocket, flicked it on.

In the darker recesses of the factory, eyes glittered when he shone his light. But they were small eyes, probably belonging to a rat, and when the little creature turned and scampered back into the far shadows, I knew it had definitely been a member of the rodent family.

Still, I felt alert and uneasy. I closed my eyes, stilled my breathing (trying, and failing, to calm my rapidly beating heart; I've never been a fan of abandoned, spooky places) and *listened*.

Again, that singing. It was the sweet, soprano female voice, lilting a wordless melody. The voice seemed to waft from everywhere and nowhere; it surrounded me, making it impossible to locate its origin. Was someone here in the building with us? I doubted that anyone would have left a music player here tuned in to the Enya station.

We ventured forward a few more steps, just as I felt the presence in front of us rise.

There was a hole in the floor a few feet ahead, a vast chasm that showed the water pipes below and led down into what was once probably a basement. One of the pipes lay open and broken, the water flowing through said basement at a very low level, sluggish and slow. As I looked down through the break, I thought I saw a shadow…

Burt turned the flashlight to the break in the pipe, and a pair of eyes—large eyes this time—shone in the beam.

I couldn't believe what I was seeing: pale green skin covered something skeletal and scaly, something slowly crawling out of the pipe to stare up at us. I…thought it was a woman. But no… Only part of it was a woman. The being had long green hair, and long sharp teeth protruded from a wide mouth, but the lower half of its body was most certainly not woman-shaped. At all. Possibly it was part…reptile?

Or fish? Either way, the lower body was sinuous and slick, and coupled with the long, claw-like arms, the overall sight was a nightmarish vision, like nothing I had ever seen or imagined. But I knew—by instinct, I guess—what it was *supposed* to be: a mermaid.

Burt and I stared down at it, and it stared up at us, and, so slowly that I thought I must be imagining it, it distended its jaw and—quite a bit like a cat—hissed at us. It was low, that sound, but it made my skin crawl, and I stepped back away from the hole. The thing below us—the mermaid—was much bigger than a human, probably twice as tall as me, if you counted the tail, and it wasn't that far from us, only ten feet or less.

"What is it?" I asked Burt, because I wanted to hear him say it. I wanted to be sure. Actually, I wanted him to prove me wrong, because *this* couldn't be a mermaid. Not this...

Burt shook his head slowly with a slight shrug, switching the flashlight off. The creature blinked, then lowered itself, coiling its scaly part beneath it, as if it might, at any moment, spring.

"I think we're in a mess of trouble," said Burt in a very small, low voice.

I took a deep breath. Granted, I didn't have much (or *any*) experience with sharp-toothed, monstrous mermaids, but I'm not a sit-there-and-do-nothing kind of witch, either. I put my hands out before me and brought up a shield of protection as quickly as I could spin it, and I felt the energy crackle about me.

Psychic protection was all well and good, but some physical protection was always a good idea, too. I picked up a tree branch that had helpfully fallen through a window at some point in the recent past, and I brandished it in front of me. Burt was fishing around in his pocket, but when he drew out his hand, all it held was a pen.

The creature cocked its head, flicked its eyes from us to the wall it would have to climb to reach us. And then, like the stuff of nightmares, it slithered off of the pipe, down over the water-covered floor of the basement, and placed its long, sharp fingers on the wall, digging claws into the metal, making it shriek. Inexplicably—but probably magically—the mermaid began to climb.

"Oh, crap," I said, which really didn't cover my horror. This was *way* beyond my area of expertise, and, honestly, I'd never hurt anything larger than a gnat, but I figured I might have some sort of fighting chance, if Burt could be helpful. The poor guy was trying, but he'd just tripped on a larger, non-wieldable branch, falling backwards into a small pile of leaves; he was currently scrabbling as he tried to rise and find his lost glasses at the same time.

It was so sudden, how the thing peered up and over the edge of the hole, that I felt my heart throw itself against my ribs. One clawed hand came over the edge, and then two, and then it was heaving itself up, jaw open too large—like a snake trying to swallow something bigger than its throat. A hiss mingled with a high-pitched, musical song that I had, before I'd known where it was coming from, thought lovely.

So, upon waking this morning, brandishing a stick at a really angry mermaid had not been on my list of things to do. But here I was, so I held the stick a little higher, shot a prayer of holy-hell-I-need-a-little-help-here to the Goddess, and braced myself.

And I felt something...changing.

I raised my head but didn't dare remove my eyes from the creature's eyes as it drew closer. And then, all at once, the mermaid sort of flew to the side, tumbling end over end as a wolf ran into it. Or rather, *on*to it.

A wolf...

It was a wolf.

My wolf.

Morgan in her wolf form (I recognized her from the markings around her muzzle, and the tuft of white fur on her tail) bit down into the thing's neck, eliciting a shriek that shattered the rest of the glass in the place, bringing me to my knees, hands clamped over my ears. Somehow, the mermaid slithered away from her, and it began circling her, its long, fish-like tail twitching. It moved like a snake, and it was dripping green ichor out of a hole in its neck. Where the fluid fell, the flooring sizzled.

Morgan was a large wolf, but she was dwarfed by the angry creature. Not that that deterred her. As I brandished my stick again, Morgan growled, hackles high, and snapped at the creature's tail, keeping it moving. It was being cowed and gradually backed away from her, towards that hole in the floor. I held the stick a little higher, and when the mermaid tried to crawl away from the wolf and away from the hole in the floor, I waved my stick threateningly.

It hissed at me, its teeth glittering wickedly in the light that shone through the hole in the roof. It wouldn't turn its back on the wolf, and it wouldn't turn its back on me, so as it writhed backwards, it half-fell, half-climbed back down into the basement. It sat growling at us in the water for a long moment, but Morgan was having none of it: she snarled, the sound ricocheting around the enclosed space. At this, the mermaid backed slowly into the pipe, disappearing from view, its hiss fading around us to nothingness.

I felt the tension leave me all at once as the adrenaline leaked out of me. I let the stick drop, and Burt stood, brushed off the knees of his jeans, wincing as he straightened. I retrieved his glasses from the ground and placed them in his hands.

Still feeling the aftershocks of heart-against-ribs, I watched Morgan as she trotted over to us, licking her lips and shaking like a very wet dog after a particularly violent rainstorm. She sat down, yawned hugely, then looked at me with imploring eyes.

I knelt down beside her, awkwardly patting the top of her head. Her wolf rolled its eyes at me, and she dog-laughed, opening her mouth wide and shaking her head. She was amused, definitely. Maybe I shouldn't have patted her head. She glanced to Burt.

"I'm fine, Morgan. Thanks for asking," he said, picking up his baseball cap from where it had fallen and placing it back on his head. He smiled at her. "Got here just in the nick of time, didn't you?"

If a werewolf could shrug, Morgan shrugged now; then she stood and stretched. She huffed out a sigh, and before our eyes, her face became smaller, her nose less elongated, her fur growing back into her body…

She transformed into a human.

Morgan stood before us, utterly naked.

"I don't have any clothes around here, see," she said, arms draped over her breasts and pelvic area. Burt didn't look phased at all as he glanced mildly at the hole in the ceiling, but I wasn't nearly as cool. A blush began to rise in me as I stared at the impossibly beautiful woman before me, at the curve of her muscles, at the curve of her breasts.

I would like to point out, again, that she was standing in front of us *naked*. Again, she seemed amused by my reaction, chuckling a little before she became serious. "And all this time, I'd been blaming poor Ellie's kids, and it was a *mermaid*. Ah, well. I'm glad nothing too serious happened, and no one got hurt. I've never heard of a mermaid coming in this far from the sea. I mean, we're not *that* far out, but still…"

"True, but what I don't understand is how the town let her in. The protections should have caught her, stopped her," sighed Burt, shrugging. "I'll have to bring this up with your father."

"Yeah—he'll get to the bottom of it," said Morgan with a soft smile. She turned to me, inclining her head and dropping her voice to a low, throaty growl. "Amy…did you get hurt?"

I glanced up into her eyes, my heart hammering against my ribs. God, if Burt hadn't been there (and it was pretty damn awkward that he was, poor guy), I would have wrapped my hands over her waist, my fingers gliding over her hips, drawing her close to me, her warm body oh so close to mine, and kissed her with the fierceness that was rising in me as I stared at her.

"No," I whispered, then cleared my throat, emotion making my words low. "I didn't get hurt," I told her. Her hair was tangled in knots, bits of leaves and twigs stuck in her waves, but as she stood there, utterly confident, utterly predatory, I don't think I'd ever seen her look more lovely.

"I'm glad," she growled, and for a moment, it seemed that she wanted to say something more, but she took a deep breath, then sighed, the smile tugging at the corners of her mouth mischievous. "I'll see you tonight—for dinner?" she asked.

Did a naked werewolf just ask me out on a date? I grinned like a fool and nodded quickly. Yes, yes, she had. And, yes, dinner would be *wonderful.*

She took one step closer, leaned down and brushed her warm, soft lips against my cheek, such a gentle, unexpected gesture that a shiver coursed through me. Then she winked at me again, and, taking a step back, she began to change. It was so surreal, watching the fur drift out of her skin, watching her skeleton morph and change, and almost instantaneously, there was a great big wolf in front of me, where Morgan the human had once stood.

She shook her pelt, licked her snout, and with a little wolfish smile, turned and trotted out of the building.

My blush deepened, my breath came short, and my heart was in danger of bolting out of my chest.

Part of me thought: *I could totally have managed by myself. I could have kicked that mermaid's butt (if she'd had one, and not a fish's tail). I hope it doesn't come back, but — if it does — I'll be ready for it!*

Another part of me thought: *That was like something out of a storybook. Except a knight in shining armor didn't save the day; a lady knight in shaggy coat and paws came to my rescue...*

The first part of me countered: *That is the most unfeminist thought I've ever thought.*

The second part only laughed: *Yeah, but you have to admit — it was ridiculously hot.*

But how did Morgan know we were in trouble?

"I hope that thing doesn't come back," said Burt, edging to the rim again and peering into the hole the mermaid had disappeared within.

"Yeah," I said, only half-listening. I brushed my fingers against my cheek where Morgan had kissed me.

Dear goddess, I had it bad.

Chapter 9: The Date

"So, you had the situation under control and could have dealt with it by yourself, but a Sapphic lady-love saved you... Hmm. Yes, that's still feminist," said Winnie nodding.

I almost snorted coffee out of my nose. "Did you *really* just say 'Sapphic lady-love?'" I chuckled and shook my head as I set my coffee cup down on the edge of the bathroom sink. "Honestly, Miss Ghost, I don't know how much credibilty you have on this subject," I teased her. "Didn't you wear corsets in your day?" I asked, putting mascara on my lashes.

"*I* didn't wear a corset," said Winnie primly. "I promise you," she said with a wink then, "there were many of us who did not. We were, after all, the *first* feminists!"

"Such a rebel," I chuckled with a shake of my head. I screwed the cap back on the mascara and studied my makeup job in the mirror.

I hadn't known Morgan for that long, but during the time that I had, I'd come to realize... Well. There's no delicate way to say this, so I should just go ahead and say it: I was *fairly* certain that I was falling in love with Morgan.

She was kind, generous, unspeakably attractive, thoughtful, intelligent beyond belief, had the most ridiculous (and wonderful) sense of humor, liked many of the same things I did...and, let's not forget that most important of all things: *she was fine with the fact that I was a witch.* That...had never happened to me before.

She was, of course, fine with the fact that I was a witch because she, herself, was a *werewolf.* But other than the likely necessity of extra vacuuming (because I assumed she shed a little), I hadn't gathered any drawbacks to that yet.

"How do I look?" I asked Winnie, turning before my ghost companion.

She cocked her head to the side, sized me up with her burning, fiery eyes and sighed. "I guess you'll do. It wouldn't be my first choice."

I chuckled again and shrugged, turning this way and that in the mirror. I was wearing a long-sleeved black dress over black leggings. Definitely skimpy by Victorian standards but pretty modest by today's mode of dress. I winked at her. "Be honest: it's not your favorite because this outfit doesn't include five different layers of Victorian underwear."

"Very funny," she huffed primly. "I'll have you know it was all very practical and comfortable."

"Admittedly, it was probably a bit more comfy than those corsets." I winked, dabbing a bit of perfume oil on my pulse points. The rush of scent made me smile; it was patchouli and rose, a blend I'd mixed myself a few new moons ago. The perfume was aging nicely, I decided, sniffing my wrist. If I closed my eyes, it made me think of...

A knock at the door. Morgan.

I almost tripped over my shoes in my haste to answer it. I could hear Winnie giggling behind me.

"Hi," I said, breathless when I opened the door. Morgan stood there, hands in her jean pockets, one hip out to the side, curving dangerously toward me, so that my breath immediately started coming a little shorter. Morgan's long, red hair was wind-ruffled and brilliantly gleaming around her face, like a halo. She wore a black leather jacket over a tight red t-shirt, and if I hadn't been leaning on the doorframe at the moment she smiled at me, her lips curling up at the corners like she was about to share a secret...I probably would have fallen to the floor, given my weakened knees.

I leaned forward, brazenly wrapped my fingers in the leather jacket's collar, drawing her close to me. Her smile deepened as she glided her hands around my waist, bringing me tightly to her, so that we pressed against one another as I lifted my chin up and kissed her hello with a fierceness that rose within me.

Winnie cleared her throat, chuckled a little and adjourned to my bedroom, leaving us alone in the doorway.

Morgan took one step back, holding me out at arm's length as she whistled lowly, her bright gaze raking up and down my length. "You look good, Amy," she murmured then, her voice a soft growl. "*Very* good."

I tucked a strand of hair behind my ear and tried to take the compliment coolly, tried *not* to turn bright red from head to toe—and failed. "Oh, this old thing," I murmured, glancing coyly into her eyes.

There was a fire burning behind her gaze. A fire that was answered deep inside of me.

She took my breath away.

Morgan held up a dark blue knapsack, tilting her head to the side a little as she said, "So, I was thinking... It's a little wild and crazy, I know, but I thought... I mean, would you like to go on a picnic with me?"

"Sounds wild and crazy," I told her with a smile, leaning forward so that I could hook the back belt loops of her jeans in my thumbs. I drew her to me so that we pressed together again. "I *like* wild and crazy," I told her softly.

"Good," she growled, and kissed me again.

I grabbed my hoodie on the way out of the apartment. We trotted down the stairs, and I was about to flick off the lights in the café when Morgan paused, reaching forward and taking my hand in hers. Only a small backlight behind the café counter was still on, but she still surveyed the place, eyes wide in the dark.

"The café looks beautiful," she told me, as she took in the new paint job, the way I'd rearrarranged everything. "You've done a really great job—you know that?" Her soft fingertips traced up my arm, making me shiver. "Your aunt's going to love this. You've done wonders in such little time. It's like you cast a spell over the place." The way she spoke those words, as if she were tasting the word "spell," made me shiver again. She was so close I could smell her skin, the orange soap she was using, the little bit of clove oil she'd dabbed on her wrists before she came to get me. It was the scent of sunshine and warmth and intoxicating possibility.

"I..." I cleared my throat a little, shifted my weight, looked up at her squarely. "You were...*really* wonderful earlier today. The way you came and saved us? Just...thank you, Morgan. I'm...not sure what that creature wanted, but I'm glad it didn't get it. Whatever it was..." I was sounding like a complete idiot, talking fast, but I could see her face outlined in the remaining low sunshine in the western sky and that one lone bulb behind the counter. The way she watched me, the curve of her lips, that smile...she was positively glowing.

She shrugged nonchalantly, eyebrows up. "I mean, it was no big deal," she said, her head to the side as her smile turned impish. We both knew that it was, in fact, a very, *very* big deal. "I was just close by and smelled something nasty — kinda like something rotting, with salt added to it. Totally unnatural for the factory site, so I came investigating. I knew Burt was distressed about the water situation again, anyway, the way those pipes were always getting clogged. It was just happy serendipity that I came when I did. I'm glad I could help out." Her brow was furrowed now as she gazed at me. "I'm glad it didn't hurt you," she said in a husky whisper, emotion making the words tense.

I shifted, felt my blood rise again. "Was it...was it really a mermaid?" I managed.

"Well..." She rocked back on her heels, shrugged a little. "I'm not sure, but if I'd have to guess, I'd say yes." She reached around me and flicked off the light, brushing past my shoulder. She kept her arm around me and gently pulled me closer to her as we walked toward the front door. "We've had lots of...*odd* stuff come through here lately," she said thoughtfully. "Which shouldn't be the case. Wolf Town has protections in place to ward off anything or anyone with negative intentions. Burt's worried that the town is getting lax on its protections. The energies feel a little weaker to me, but I don't know why. I've got to talk to Dad about it."

We went out into the soft, purple twilight, the clouds drifting along the edge of the horizon a myriad of colors that blended beautifuly with the brilliant red maple trees lining the main street of Wolf Town. The sun drifted low, ready to sink below the edge of the world, and the air was filled with the symphony of autumn insects. It was much too warm for an October evening, was, in fact, a bit like an Indian Summer. I remembered those from when I was a kid, when it was hot in October, when I ran around outside in my t-shirt and little witchy skirts, trying to spot fairies.

"See? It was far too nice to stay indoors," said Morgan companionably. But the way that she looked at me, her grin almost wolfish, made me shiver again, in the best possible way.

"Okay, wait a minute, though," I said, one brow raised as I smiled devilishly at her. "I've read all of my fairy tales. Should I really be going into the woods with a wolf?" I asked her, laughing a little as we began to walk behind the Witch's Way Cafe, towards the bordering forest. The leaves were the perfect, burning color, and they crunched beneath our feet like music.

"That depends, Little Red Riding Hood," said Morgan, arching a brow. "After all," she said mildly, "isn't it true that most of the wolves in fairy stories are easily outsmarted?"

I snorted. "You're smart."

"They're not fast enough," she said, her voice going lower, into a playful growl.

"I have a feeling you're very fast," I told

her, my heartbeat quickening.

"But, according to fairy tales, bad wolves never win," she said, spreading her hands, looking up as the branches arched over our heads, swallowing us into the golden woods. She cast a backward glance at me, her lips turned up at the corners as she held out her hand. I placed my hand in her warm palm, and when our skin touched, I shivered again.

"Okay—but what about good wolves?" I asked her, as she helped me over a fallen tree limb. I paused, looked up into her eyes, feeling my pulse pounding at our little teases.

"I've never read a *good* wolf story," said Morgan, voice low as she drew me closer, one warm arm wrapped about my waist. "But I suppose they end like all good fairy tales do: with a happily ever after."

Heatbeat pounding through me, I leaned forward against her, capturing her mouth with my own.

She gripped me tighter, and need began to race through me. We were on the edge of the woods, still in sight of the town, and how naughty was I really feeling? I didn't want our first time to be against a tree.

(Or did I *totally* want it to be against a tree?)

(And, wow, I was thinking about our *first time*. Because, at this rate, it was going to be happening very, *very* soon.)

138

Morgan had such a wildness to her, a great grace and beauty that made me feel, when I was in her company, as if anything was possible. She wanted me, and I wanted her, and that attraction between us was like fire, eating the both of us up, consuming us utterly.

When Morgan broke away, I felt a little disappointed...until I realized that there was a woman walking her dog along the sidewalk not that far from us. If it was, in fact, even a dog. The thing was about as big as...well, a wolf.

We cleared our throats, held hands and began to enter the woods. As I put my other hand (still tingling from how hard I'd gripped her) in my hoodie pocket, I realized my hoodie was, in fact, red.

As if she'd heard my thoughts, Morgan grinned sidelong at me. "You really are Little Red Riding Hood," she said with a low chuckle, drawing me close to her as we walked together. As we ventured further along the broad, well-groomed path, a leaf fell in front of us, settling in a mosaic of reds and golds on the forest floor. It was such a perfect, autumn evening, and my heart was practically bursting with gratitude.

Again, just as if she could hear what I was thnking, Morgan brushed her shoulder against mine. "This makes me happy," she said, squeezing my hand, looking up at the colorful treetops that waved back and forth, back and forth, in the warm October wind. "*You* make me happy," she added after a long moment, and she looked down at me when she said it, eyes greener for being surrounded by the red of the forest, the bright red of her hair. Her gaze flashed with a deep intensity that my entire body answered.

"Me, too," I whispered, squeezing her hand.

We walked along the path, crunching through small piles of leaves that had gathered along the edges of the path, until we found a small clearing at the side of the pathway, perfectly carved into the tall, surrounding pines like it was meant for walkers to sit here and have a rest.

"Let's picnic here!" Morgan said, gesturing to the leaf pile on the edge of the clearing. It looked pretty comfy to me, and I smiled, nodding. Morgan drew a loud fleecy blanket out of the knapsack (it had about every color you could ever imagine in a joyful, non-matching plaid print), and together we spread it on the ground. I sank down on one edge of it, and she on the other, and together we devoured the blocks of cheese, crackers and grapes she'd packed, sharing two metal containers of a surprisingly sweet tea.

"How much sugar did you put in this?" I chuckled, taking another sip.

"About a cup," she said thoughtfully, then deepened her smile, her eyes flashing. She leaned forward a little as she lowered her voice: "I happen to like sweet things," she practically purred.

My heartbeat roared through me, along with a chuckle. "Oh, you didn't!" I laughed, giggling. "That's so cheesy!"

She flopped down on her stomach, stretching out and lying on the blanket, pillowing her head easily in my lap. The gesture was so intimate that I bit my lip, didn't even think: I reached out and gently began to stroke her fiery hair. We were still learning the comforts of being together, the little ways we could touch, the warmth of having each other close. Her hair was so soft, smelling of coconut today. I wanted to put my nose to it, my mouth, touching my skin to the soft place on her neck, just beneath her ear, kissing her there...

She sighed contentedly, her eyes closed. "This is nice," she said.

"Yeah," I murmured, brushing my thumb along the side of her cheek. Her skin was so soft, so warm, and there was something building inside of me, something that was lit and wouldn't burn out, a need that was rising.

She felt it, too. I know she did. Her voice cracked a little as she cleared her throat and said, "You know, people outside of Wolf Town considered these woods to be haunted, long ago. Some still think they are."

I paused, my palm against her cheek as I

felt my mood darken, shuddering a little, remembering the fairy court. I hoped she didn't notice the shift. "It doesn't *feel* haunted," I said quietly, which was the truth, and she nodded, opened her eyes and gazed up at me.

"Yeah, it's not haunted. I think people said it was because we went hunting in these woods so much. As wolves. And, I mean, Wolf Town has a weird reputation. A lot of people avoid it because of what they say lives here."

"Oh, really?" I asked, raising a brow as I gazed down at her. "And what, exactly, do they say lives here?"

"Oh, the usual suspects," she said, rolling her eyes with a small, tight shrug. "Fairies and witches and warlocks and representatives of the devil. You know good old New England and its preoccupation with the devil," she said, with a sigh. "Surprisingly, the people who rail on and on about the evil residents of Wolf Town don't mention wolves all that often. Wolf Town is a small town surrounded by many small towns that are prone to gossip."

I sighed, sat back on my hands as she rolled back over onto her stomach, resting her chin on her palm beside me, the full length of her body pressing against my right thigh.

"Your mention of witches reminds me of something, actually," I told her, frowning a little. "The full moon esbat is coming up, and I don't have anything planned for it. I've been too busy."

"Esbat?" she asked, brow furrowed. "What's that?"

"Oh…" I tilted my head. "Witches call the full and new moon days Esbats. They're like Sabbats, the witches' high holy days, but a bit smaller. We normally perform rituals on them. When I was back home, my mom always invited over her coven, and everyone danced around in the living room and then drank margaritas afterward. It was a spiritual, wonderful party. A really great time." I shrugged a little. "Witches typically do either group work or solitary work in their spiritual lives. I always thought I loved solitary work, but now I *have* to be solitary and…" I sighed. "Anyway, it's not a big deal. I'll come up with something simple to do."

Morgan thought for a long moment before she asked, her voice low, "What do you do at a witch's ritual?"

I drew up my knees, clasped my hands around my legs, tucking my skirt under my toes as I pressed my thigh against her shoulder. She was so warm, and as her arm curled around me, drawing me even closer, I melted against her side, her laying on her stomach on the ground, me seated beside her, so naturally, as if we did this all the time. "Well," I said quietly, taking her hand in my own and turning it over so that her palm was open to the sky. I placed my index finger against the skin of her palm and slowly traced a circle there as I held her eyes. "The first thing you do," I whispered, "is you cast the circle."

"Cast the circle…" she said, voice low and strained as she held my gaze, her eyes burning. I continued to trace the circle on her palm.

"You draw a circle about yourself for protection. That means you visualize a circle made of glowing white light around you. You call to the four directions and their elements to come and help you—north is earth, et cetera. And then, you ask the Goddess to come and help you in the rite, too. You meditate, sometimes, or you raise energy. You usually do all of this for a specific reason. Like, for a full moon esbat, you usually go along with what the moon stands for." I pressed my palm down against hers as I smiled. "October's full moon is called the Blood Moon. So, blood is a metaphor for the waning life and the world drifting toward winter. You do a ritual to honor that, honor the turning of the wheel of the year…" I drifted off, reached down and gently tucked a stray curl of red behind her ear, letting my fingertips brush over her cheek. I was rewarded with a hitch of breath, and her gazing at me with impassioned eyes.

She sat up then, leaned closer to me as she gathered my hands, interlacing her long fingers with my own. She cleared her throat a little as she held my gaze. "What does it take to make a group? Like — one, plus at least one more?"

I nodded.

"So." She said in a low growl, "What if I joined you for your ritual? I mean, if you'd have me, of course."

"What?" I blinked. "You'd want to do a ritual with me?"

"I'm fascinated by all of this," she whispered, leaning closer as her eyes sparked. "It seems like a beautiful religion," she murmured sincerely. "And, I mean, I'm all about universal energies, but I've never really had anything spiritual in my life. I admire how it's such a part of *your* life," she said, smiling softly. "But I don't want to intrude, or be...you know...*that* girlfriend..."

Girlfriend? A thrill ran through me.

I squeezed her hand, our fingers spread and interlaced so efforlessly. "Thank you..." I said quietly, holding her gaze. She cocked her head, and I swallowed, continued, "Thank you for being so openminded about all of this, for being so interested. It means a lot to me."

"Yes, well," she whispered, voice husky, "the pleasure is all mine."

We leaned towards each other, our mouths close, and we were about to kiss when Morgan glanced up and down the continuing trail, lifting her head, sniffing the air. She stood abruptly then, nose pointing up to the heavens as she inhaled deeply.

I stood with her, brushing off the bottom of my skirt and watching her, perplexed, until she took my hand again, tugged at me, grinning toothily. "This is *awesome*," she said, pulling me behind her as she set off down the path. "You're going to *love* this!"

I chuckled at how delighted she was as she coaxed me along, first walking quite quickly, then trotting, then running. When we stopped, it was so suddenly that I skidded into her with an *oof*.

"Sorry," she whispered, placing her arm around me tightly and pressing her finger against my lips in the universal *shh* sign. Then, holding my gaze with raised brows, she pointed slowly ahead of us.

In front of us spread a natural clearing in the woods. A few trees had fallen, offering an opening to the sky among the rest of the forest, already radiant with the setting sun. Virulent crimson and passionate indigo mixed together with rays of sweet orange. It was one of the most intoxicating sunsets I'd ever seen, but that's not what Morgan was pointing toward.

There, in the forest clearing, was light. White light, silvered light, that pooled across the ground as if by magic. In the center, across the soft buffalo grasses, drifted human shapes that didn't seem to touch the ground. They were ephemeral, amorphous, and I might have thought they were ghosts if not for the impressive furl of colors that grew from their shoulders.

Wings.

They were fairies.

I gave a sharp intake of breath when I realized what they were, but almost at the same moment, a calming sensation swept through me. These were not the tall, imposing fairies who had ordered me to deliver a piece of mail. These fairies were, in fact, so far removed from that dark fairy court, they seemed like different beings entirely. They drifted across the grass, amorphous and brightly colored, as light and airy as gauze. I felt at ease, soothed, as if I had nothing to worry about.

They drifted together in a wide, irregular circle, almost touching one another with the tips of their wings. They turned, and they moved, spiraling, twirling...dancing, I realized. Morgan and I watched as, together, they clasped hands, and, while the last sliver of sun sank below the edge of the world, the fairies began to dance together in a circle, whirling together, one moment slow and stately, the next wild and frenzied with joy.

They spun, and as we watched, I began to hear it—faint at first, but gradually filling the clearing with harmony. This music was actually similar to the mermaid's song, but lighter and clearer sounding, women's voices raised in a soft, airy song that conveyed none of the undercurrent of menace in the mermaid's melody.

So the fairies danced and sang together, spinning in an ever-widening circle, quicker and quicker until they moved too fast for me to make out individual wings. And as the first star peeked out between folds of velvet blue overhead, the fairies—all of them—disappeared in a flashing wink. Gone.

I breathed out, realizing I'd been holding my breath for the past minute. I panted, hand over my heart, as I closed my eyes and still saw the fairy circle there, still spinning, wings bright and arched and beautiful beyond my most fanciful imaginings.

"Oh, my goddess..." I whispered then, opening my eyes and looking to Morgan. I was crying, but I didn't even care, wiping away my tears silently as, holding hands tightly, we both moved into the clearing, gliding as slowly as if we were walking into a dream.

There, on the ground, where the fairies had danced, was a perfect round ring of mushrooms. I crouched down, brushed my fingertips across the blades of grass ringing one small mushroom reverently. I glanced back up at Morgan, who was smiling gently down at me. "How...how did you know they were here?" I breathed. "That's...that's..." Nothing I could say would convey what I was feeling, so I fell silent, hand pressed to the ground.

"I smelled something lovely," she said, crouching down beside me. "I've seen them before. I know what they smell like. Like perfect wildflowers, out of season." She held my gaze. "I had to share that with you," she said, voice low.

"Thank you," I whispered, and she leaned forward and kissed me.

When Morgan kissed me, it sent a tingle through me, from the very tips of my purple-painted toenails right up to the very top of my head. A rush moved through me, and I felt her warmth, felt her heat come from the deepest parts of her to eat me up—much like a wolf, I supposed. She placed her hands at the curve of my waist, around my shoulders, and she drew me to her closer, tighter, fiercer, and I put my own arms about her neck and drew her to *me*, my heart burning bright and devouring her as much as she devoured me.

When she kissed me in that moment, I knew that I wanted her, wanted her because I'd just seen something so beautiful that I could not explain it, something so beautiful that I already saw reflected in her when she smiled at me or told a ridiculously corny joke or came to my rescue to save me from a not-so-little mermaid. I wanted her, she wanted me, and that want was perfect.

But I wanted our first time to be perfect,

too.

Okay, so I guess I *am* a little old-fashioned in that respect. I'm not the kind of woman who has to wait months and months before having sex with her girlfriend. But the first time *does* have to be pretty darn near perfect. As I kissed her deeply in the autumn twilight, right next to the circle where fairies had just danced...I realized that I knew the perfect moment.

The Esbat was tomorrow. If Morgan was really going to come and do the ritual with me... I would make a perfect dinner. I would light the perfect candles.

And, together, we would make the perfect night.

Excitement and heat raced through me as I broke the kiss, as I backed away a little and held Morgan's gaze, her gaze filled with the same want and need that was roaring through me.

But I had a strange feeling, too. There was a pricking along the back of my neck, and I straightened, turning my head.

"What's the matter?" asked Morgan, instantly on alert, frowning as she stared past me, at the darkening woods.

I frowned a little, too, as I straightened, as I reached up and absentmindedly rubbed the back of my neck. "Nothing," I told her with a small shrug. "Hey," I ventured, trying to keep my voice steady. "Do you smell anything else with your, um, great wolfy powers?" I tried to tease her, but my voice was too high. She was staring at me with narrowed eyes. "Is there anyone else around?" I said, to clarify.

She turned to look past me again, raising her nose a little into the chill wind that had begun to blow.

"I just smell wolves," she said gently, placing her arm around my waist and drawing me close. "It's the smell of Wolf Town. There's no one else there."

I tried to think about tomorrow night as we walked, arm in arm, back toward the Witch Way Café. I tried to think about what I would cook, how I would set up the ritual space...

But all the way home, the hair on the back of my neck remained raised.

Still...it was probably nothing.

Chapter 10: The Ritual

Saturday morning dawned, brilliant and perfect. I opened my bedroom window and sat on a cushion on the floor for several long moments, head pillowed on my arms on the sill as I watched the sun come up over the edge of the world, golden beyond belief.

I felt golden, too, as I got dressed, layering my favorite swishy black skirt with a thin purple sweater. Black and purple—it's a thing. My favorite silver pentacle clasped around my neck on a thin silver chain, a splash of pumpkin-scented perfume on my wrists, and I dashed out into the living room, putting my shoes on over purple- and black-striped socks.

"Where are you headed to?" asked Winnie, peeking up and over the edge of her see-through book from where she floated, about a foot above the comfy, plush chair in the corner.

"It's Farmer's Market day!" I told her with a wide smile as I bounced around on one foot, toeing my other foot into my favorite black flats. "I am about to pay a ridiculous amount of money for bars of soap that have interesting names and that smell out of this world. I'm also going to clean the stalls out of reasonably priced vegetables," I grinned at her, gathering my cloth bags into one larger cloth bag and slinging the strap over my shoulder.

"I'd like to point out that you have a very impressive soap collection already," said Winnie, with one brow raised. "I mean, I've never *seen* that much soap in one place before. At least forty bars. Not that I ever spent five minutes of my afterlife counting them—"

"I have a handmade soap addiction," I nodded seriously. I told her goodbye and trotted down the steps through the Witch Way Café, and out into Wolf Town itself.

Outside, as early as it was, the townsfolk of Wolf Town were flooding the streets in anticipation of the Farmer's Market. Morgan had told me about it excitedly, how usually the Wolf Town Farmer's Market was only a summer thing, with one exception: the weekend before the weekend before the Halloween Carnival, making it—essentially—the beginning of the Halloween festivities here in Wolf Town. That this year's autumnal Farmer's Market fell on a full moon was just too perfect, and it tickled me pink.

Speaking of colors, the woman who'd just walked past me down the sidewalk was wearing a multicolored plaid mini-skirt. It was retro and fabulous, but my brow furrowed as I stood there for a long moment. That skirt reminded me of something...

Wait. Plaid... Morgan's plaid blanket. I paused at the edge of the Witch Way Cafe and peered around the building's wall, looking past it and into the brightening forest. We'd left our things in the woods before we dashed off to see fairies dancing... We'd forgotten to go back for them.

Had that even happened? Had any of it happened? The fairies, Morgan... It seemed like a perfect dream.

I sighed, stowed my cloth bags in the Witch Way Cafe's mailbox. I couldn't just leave the blanket, the Tupperware, and Morgan's knapsack there. I had completely forgotten about it until now, and I can only assume Morgan did, too...

"Good morning, Amy!" called Victor from his morning walk, making the rounds of the town. It was more of a casual stroll than exercise, and he was reading the morning paper on his phone while doing it, surprisingly—and gracefully—not running into things. But he *was* a vampire, and I supposed vampires, out of all creatures, were pretty darn graceful.

"Good morning!" I called to him, turning to go down the small alley and into the forest.

"Where are you headed?" he asked, pausing in front of the café and peering at me curiously.

"I'm going out to the woods—" I

gestured.

"Not to the Ninth Order?" His brows rose. "I happen to know that your lady love will be crushed that you said good morning to the trees before her," he said, winking. I blushed a little. Then he cleared his throat. "You know," he murmured, leaning down, lowering his voice to a conspirator's whisper, "she really fancies you."

"Well...I fancy *her*," I told him with a small smile. What was he getting at? The tone of his voice hadn't been spectacularly warm.

"I mean...she's had her heart broken before." When he looked at me, it was with a raised eyebrow.

"Victor, if you're giving me the 'don't break her heart' speech," I told him with a chuckle and a raised eyebrow of my own, "I promise you, I have absolutely no intention of doing that." I was relieved that this was all he was implying. Of course I had no intention of breaking Morgan's heart.

But he wasn't done yet. He cleared his throat again, glanced past my shoulder out toward the forest.

"There has been an ill wind blowing from the woods and around Wolf Town lately," he said, inclining his head in the direction I'd planned to take. "I'm...worried." His eyes gazed into my own, unwavering. "Amy, I know that you're a witch, and that you must be a strong witch if you're of the Linden line. Hell, even *vampires* have heard of the Lindens." He grimaced, turned, looked at the sun as it began to scale the sky.

I waited patiently, my heart flip-flopping in my chest, beginning to beat quicker. For whatever reason, I remembered the bad feeling that I'd had in the forest last night. But nothing had happened then. I had nothing to worry about, right? It was just a silly, baseless feeling...

"Wolf Town brings the people to it that it needs," he said then, pressing his lips together into a small frown. "It brought you. I know you're needed. If...anything happens..." He trailed off, waved his hands helplessly. "Morgan... Well. Just look after her, okay? She's a really good person."

Was he asking me to protect her? *Her*? The werewolf? I was just a human woman. I mean, look at my recent run-in with the mermaid. It hadn't been *me* that the creature had backed away from.

And what in the world would a *werewolf* need protecting from?

I stared at Victor, mystified, but nodded. "I'll help her in whatever way I can. Should anything happen," I whispered, feeling my skin prick again, like it had last night. I shivered. "Victor..." I began, wondering what the hell this could be about, but he shook his head, cast his eyes to the woods, and, very carefully and slowly, brought a single finger up to his lips.

Victor's mouth formed a downward curving line, and he seemed to want to say something more, but he straightened, nodded. "Have fun in the woods, Amy," he said then, with false brightness. "Consider stopping by the Ninth Order after your work." And he continued down the street sedately, as only a vampire can walk, glancing down at his phone again as if nothing odd had transpired between us.

I stood in front of the café, the hairs on the back of my neck standing at attention as I tried to make sense of what he'd just said. But that's the thing: it *didn't* make sense. With a frown, I tucked that very weird conversation into my heart to mull over later and ventured into the alley beside the Witch Way Café, and then out back and into the woods, lost in my thoughts.

The space beneath the trees felt light and airy today, the shadows of the previous night dispelled with the mist. A flock of crows danced on their wings above the branches, and it was easy enough to find Morgan's blanket and knapsack and Tupperware of uneaten crackers, left untouched by the forest animals *probably* because it smelled like a wolf. I lifted and shook off the blanket into the morning air.

What had Victor been talking about? The uneasiness circled my chest, even as I tried to push it away.

I paused, folding the blanket over my arm, knapsack in hand. He'd said an ill wind had been blowing in from the woods. I glanced around me, but of course I saw nothing unusual—just a gorgeous New England forest in full autumn mode. Still, though, I shivered as I turned to go.

As I walked the forest path, back out into the meadow and toward the Witch Way Café, I happened to glance down at my feet. There, spreading out and away from me, was a patch of clover. It was nothing spectacular—clover grew everywhere—but as I knelt down, feeling the familiar tingle of good energies fill me, pushing away my bad feeling, I plucked one of the plants and held it up to the light.

A patch of four-leaf clover, right along the edge of town. The good magic was still here, still strong in Wolf Town. It filled me with comfort. No matter what was going on with that fairy court, no matter what bad feelings I had...there was still a patch of four-leaf clovers right here.

That *had* to be a good sign.

I grabbed the cloth bags back out of the mailbox, and—carrying the blanket, knapsack and bags—made my way down the sunlit sidewalk in Wolf Town, toward the coffee shop.

"Hello, beautiful," said Morgan, when I entered the Ninth Order. She'd been wiping off one of the tables closest to the door, but she dropped her rag on the tabletop, turned, and with strong arms, swept me up and twirled me like I weighed five pounds. She held me tightly to her as she kissed me fiercely.

She'd called me *beautiful*. My toes curled in pleasure.

"You'll have to forgive me if I roll my eyes," called Victor from behind the counter. "I'll do my best to keep it to a minimum of five eyerolls per minute, but you guys are just too much," he chuckled. He seemed totally back to normal now and way less ominous than earlier, like our conversation really *had* never happened.

"Then don't watch," said Morgan imperiously, and she leaned forward and kissed me again, her mouth pressing against mine.

I pressed my forehead to hers as she grabbed my hand and tugged me toward the counter, probably to make me a latte, when I managed to take in the fact that the Ninth Order was very full of customers this morning. Not abnormal, especially with the Farmer's Market going on. But everyone was dressed up in costumes...again. *Most* of the customers were wearing moonwalking suits this time. There were only a few in *Star Trek* uniforms.

"*Another* alien convention?" I marveled, sitting at the closest table to the counter. Morgan began making my pumpkin latte, steaming the soy milk with a smile.

"Yeah... You'd be surprised. Alien

conventions happen pretty often in Wolf Town," said Morgan, exchanging a glance with Victor.

"When does the Farmer's Market open?" I asked, furrowing my brow as I watched them exchange that look. "Ten? Nine?"

"Nine," said Morgan. She stalked out from behind the counter and set the latte down in front of me, tugging out the adjacent chair with a toe and sitting on it backwards as she watched me with a wolfish grin. I smiled at her and sat still for a blissful moment, inhaling the steam of that delicious-smelling latte.

"A perfect ten," I whispered to her, sipping at the cup in what I hoped was a suggestive manner. I burned my tongue.

Victor rolled his eyes—for the fifth time.

"You gonna go to the market with her?" he asked Morgan, who looked at the clock and nodded, taking off her apron as she leaned back in her chair.

"Surely you don't need me?" she asked the vampire with a wry smile and a wink. He sighed and glanced over the ridiculously packed coffee shop.

"No, I should be totally fine," he said, voice flat. But then he shook his head with a smile. "They all ordered already, anyway. You're set. You kids go have fun," he said, wiping the steamer off with a towel.

"You're wonderful," said Morgan, tossing him a high-five into the air.

"We'll be back soon, Victor, I promise," I told him. And Morgan and I strolled out of the coffee shop arm in arm, and latte in hand.

My earlier ominous feelings had seemed to evaporate. After all, how could there be anything terrible in the world when you're falling in love?

I was so happy that it colored everything I saw: the white booths unfolded and set up before us on the sidewalks of Wolf Town; the tie-dyed skirt of the old woman who sold goat milk soaps which she placed them in rows on her starched white tabletop; the blue suspenders of an older guy who was setting up a little table with brochures on horse-riding lessons for the nearby Throne Farm. The logo for Throne Farm told the truth about the stables, however—a pegasus rampant, with stars behind its streaming mane. It was kind of indicative that Throne Farm didn't offer *normal* horseback-riding lessons...

I breathed in the scents of autumn, the soaps and the latte and the fallen leaves and the fresh-baked pies on the bakery table. I heard the sounds, the laughter and the music as a busking violin player began to tune his instrument, drawing his rosined bow over the strings. Morgan bumped her shoulder gently against mine, and when I looked up into her eyes, took in the warmth of her face, I knew something with a bone-deep knowledge, which was weird and sudden, but I knew it like the lifelines on my palms: I *belonged* here.

I belonged in Wolf Town. I was meant to be here.

And I was absolutely and utterly *meant* to be falling in love with her.

The morning was perfect, a golden, glorious set of autumn hours. Until we were on our way out of the market. The not-so-great feeling began with a little chill traveling across my right shoulder. I turned, and though we were quite distant from one another, I locked eyes with a stranger. A tall, beautiful...*odd* man. He wore silver clothes, and his hair shifted colors in the sunlight, and he leaned against a great, old oak tree on the outskirts of the Farmer's Market, practically behind the buildings. As I watched him, he stood, stretched nonchalantly, and turned and went back into the woods.

He had wings.

I rubbed at my eyes, looked again. He wasn't there. That meant nothing, of course. He could have disappeared in a flick of fairy dust, or maybe he'd never really been there at all—but I knew better. I knew, in that moment, that I had seen one of the fairy court. And he had been watching me.

"Ready to head back? Hey..."

I turned, blinked. Morgan was frowning, looking from me back to the distant tree.

"Are you all right?" she asked, stepping closer, brow furrowed in worry as her strong fingers closed around my elbow.

"Yeah," I fibbed, shaking my head.

I don't know why I didn't tell her. It was complicated, really, my reason. I had a bad feeling about her father, and who wants to tell their girlfriend that her father gives them the creeps?

And, anyway, there was probably nothing to worry about.

Probably…

I saved the apple pie we'd bought at the market for after the ritual and began to peel potatoes late in the afternoon, chopping them into large chunks, pouring veggie broth over them after browning them. My mother always made Harvest Stew for the full Blood Moon, one of the only esbats that had a specific menu in our family. For about half a minute, I actually considered making bread from scratch, but I wasn't masochistic, and I remembered I'd bought a stone-ground wheat loaf from the bakery table, along with the pie. It'd go well with dinner.

The kitchen became rife with aromas that made my mouth water. They even caught the attentions of Winifred. I'd assumed that ghosts had no sense of smell, but she wandered in now, led by her nose, exaggeratingly sniffing the air, her eyes closed happily.

"Goodness, that smells wonderful," she said and sighed, leaning against the door jamb. "But why are you going to so much trouble?"

"It's the full moon, and Morgan is coming over for a ritual and feast," I replied, stirring the stew. When I took the cover off the pot, a bellow of steam filled the air. My stomach growled loudly.

"That'll be fun," she said, sitting at the small kitchen table, covered with my purchases from the market. She hovered above the kitchen chair. "Will there be any devils involved?" she asked politely.

I rolled my eyes and cast her a sideways glance. She snickered, most unladylike, covering her mouth.

"Don't be ridiculous. And you know better," I said, covering the pot again as I brandished the ladle in her direction. "Keep this up," I told her, waggling my eyebrows, "and I'll exorcise you."

"You wouldn't dare!" she giggled, laughing. "You love me. You know it. You don't exorcise ghosts you love."

"I admit—you do provide a certain amount of company," I sniffed, but ended up grinning, sitting next to her. "Honestly? I'm a little nervous..." I confessed, picking up the white candle I'd gotten at the Market, too; it was perfect for the full moon esbat I had planned. Well, that I had *sort* of planned. I chewed on a nail distractedly.

"Don't be nervous," said Winnie, putting her see-through arm around my shoulders in loose terms. I couldn't feel her, but the gesture was appreciated. "You're going to do fine. Why are you nervous? You have absolutely nothing to be nervous about."

"She's...she's very different from my previous girlfriends," I said, peeling back a bit of wax from the candle's wick. I held the wax in my hands, so white it almost shone in the dim kitchen. "This is the big stakes now, you know?"

"No, I don't know," said Winnie, burning eyes narrowed, brows furrowed. "Tell me."

"I think she's the one," I whispered, feeling my heart pound as I said it aloud.

"The one?"

"Oh, goodness, Winnie," I said, pushing off from the table and pacing across the small kitchen. "I think she's the one for me," I said very, *very* quietly.

"Oh," she replied, and sat and thought about that for a long moment. Then she cocked her head and glanced up at me. "What makes you so sure?" It wasn't asked in an unfriendly tone: she was genuinely curious.

I sat down again, biting my lip. "I had

a...vision," I said with care, "before I came here. It showed me the Witch Way Café, and it showed me Wolf Town, and it showed me...her. And a love I'd never felt before. That I'm feeling now."

Winnie pondered this, chin in hands. "I have to admit—I sort of *see* something when you two are together," she ventured, then. "As a life-challenged person, I'm able to see that there's a glow of color, usually different colors, around all living people, but when the two of you get together, the colors change; they kind of merge. It's quite beautiful, really," she said, and smiled shyly at me. "I wish I'd had something like that when I was alive."

"Forgive my ignorance on such things," I said, leaning forward, "but, I mean, can't ghosts..." I waved my hands helplessly. "Date?"

She snorted and laughed, but then she paused. "I actually...don't know. I've never met another ghost I liked. They're mostly creepy. Or, you know, distracted, being dead and all." She tugged at the collar of her blouse and sighed.

"It's now my mission to set you up with someone of ghost-kind you might like," I said, rising to stir the stew once more. "What's your type?"

"Oh..." she said, trailing off. She shook her head. "Anyone without a pulse that might be interested in me. It's all well and good for you," she scoffed. "*You* wouldn't understand how difficult it is to find someone…"

I snorted so hard, the tea I was sipping came out of my nose. I wiped at my face with a tea towel and kept chuckling. "Oh, goddess, Winnie, you do know who you're talking to, right?" I chortled. "Come on, seriously! I'm a lesbian! Do you know how hard it is to find a woman who happens to be a lesbian, happens to be my type and who happens to be single?" I raised an eyebrow and shook my head, chuckling. "Let me just tell you that I totally understand," I told her then, placing my ladle over my heart with a nod. "Aren't there many ghosts in Wolf Town?" I asked.

"Oh, yes," she told me, nodding. "Many. And we have little get-togethers pretty frequently, for the undead. We even gather on the night of the Halloween Carnival and actually have a little ball all our own in the old Town Hall." She jerked her thumb to indicate down the road. "But it's a dreadfully boring affair. We mostly just stand around and look at our feet. We don't have music."

"Surely there are some dead guys who were once musicians," I pointed out.

She shook her head. "Not around here."

"Huh…" I thought about it. "Well, it's such a simple thing. I can totally fix that! What if I asked Allen MacRue if he would leave — oh, I don't know—maybe a radio going all night, the night of the Carnival, at the old Town Hall?"

"Really?" she asked, eyes wide.

"Absolutely," I grinned at her. "You must dance with everyone you find remotely attractive, and then tell me how it all went."

"The one ghost who I do like best happens to be headless, unfortunately," she said brightly. "But it really is more about the heart, rather than the appearance!"

I closed my mouth and blinked. "Yes," I said, trying to *not* imagine Winnie dancing with a headless horseman. "This is true." I stirred the stew once more absentmindedly, then started when I heard a knock at the door. "Oh, goodness!" I murmured, my heart beginning to beat loudly against my ribs as I practically tore off my apron, ran to the bathroom and smoothed down my hair in the mirror.

"Please," I said hurriedly, waving at Winnie as I trotted to the front door. "Please, would you give us a little space?" I asked, clasping my hands in front of me.

"What? Leave you alone for an evening?" She raised an eyebrow, wolfish grin widening her lips. "But that wouldn't be *proper*, Amy. You know us stodgey Victorians. Really, I'm more like your chaperone—"

"I might just totally rethink exorcising you!" I told her, folding my arms as I shook my head.

Winifred sighed and rolled her burning eyes. "Oh, very well, missy. But you owe me one!" she said, and she gave me a little half-bow and drifted through the apartment door, presumably through Morgan, and down and into the Witch Way Café, leaving the apartment ghost-free. And leaving me and Morgan alone to be together...in whichever way we saw fit.

I threw open the door, and there she was, fiery red hair in a cloud of scarlet about her head, her eyes sparkling as she took me in. We embraced tightly, and I inhaled the scent of her as I pressed my nose to her shoulder: sandalwood. She'd brought some wildflowers she'd picked, and she almost dropped them as she swept me up into a warm hug, closing the door behind her.

"So!" she said, dropping me down, kissing me squarely. The kiss lasted for a moment or longer as I tasted the spice and warmth of her (she tasted like coffee). She cleared her throat, smiling sideways at me as she brought the flowers up and proferred them to me. "Um...I brought you flowers," she said. "I...didn't ask you ahead of time if I should bring anything, or, you know—" She cleared her throat, spread her hands with a smooth shrug. "Dress a certain way? I asked Victor, but apparently vampire sabbats are very different from witch sabbats, and he was radically unhelpful—"

170

"You're fine," I said, hiding my blush in the blossoms as I inhaled their heady fragrance. "These are wonderful," I told her, smiling up at her. "Please! Come in! Get comfortable! I thought we'd eat after the ritual if you aren't too famished—"

"I'm fine," she said, even as her stomach growled loudly. She laughed, shook her head, put a hand over her belly. "Don't listen to it," she said, winking at me. "Truly, I'm fine." When she looked at me, her eyes were gleaming, and there was a constant smile turning up the right corner of her mouth. She looked impish, mischievous, and I wanted to melt into that, wanted to hook my thumbs in her belt loops, draw her to me strongly and kiss her again. Once more with feeling.

I could feel my cheeks blazing and, suddenly, I was self-conscious. "So," I told her softly, folding my hands in front of myself to keep them from fidgeting, from reaching out to her. "Are you ready?"

Her eyes darkened with need, but she stood tall, resolute, and nodded once.

I turned, flicked on the lights in the living room. It was just seven o'clock, but it was already dark out. I dragged the little coffee table into the center of the space just as I assumed my mother was doing at exactly the same moment. I'd made her promise not to call me tonight, had told her about my plans with Morgan. She'd screamed with delight (almost causing deafness) and had made me promise to give her all the details tomorrow. I'd agreed; she'd agreed. I hoped the evening went well enough to coo about.

I didn't really know what to expect. None of my other girlfriends had ever shown even the slightest interest in the things I did on esbats or sabbats. One of them had been completely *un*supportive, convinced for a very large portion of our dating time that I really *did* invoke demons in my rituals.

I sighed, closing my eyes, grounding myself, imagining the earth beneath me cradling me, holding me up. I spread a purple cloth over the coffee table, placed my new white candle on a little silver plate. I added my clay pentacle that I'd made when I was twelve at art class in school. It was a little misshapen, but it still made me smile. Next came the wand my mother had made for me the day I was born. She'd gathered a branch from the apple tree I'd been conceived under (a fact that had once embarrassed me, but now gave me a sense of place and gravity), wrapped in tarnished silver wire that my mother had bent around it while she labored with me. It was a little crooked, but it was filled with love.

I had no need for an athame or cauldron or the elemental candles. It would be too much, and it might overwhelm Morgan, all of those tools of my religion. I wanted to make the ritual bare bones tonight, create the thing to be simple and elegant. I rose, lit a few candles along the wall, and turned off the light in the living room. I smoothed the front of my skirt, adjusted my worn pentacle around my neck, the star shape pressing against the pad of my fingers as the familiar rush of energy from the beginning esbat filled me, now tinged with equal parts nervousness and hope. I hoped Morgan would not be *bored out of her skull*. I hoped that maybe she'd enjoy it a little.

I hoped she loved me...

I hoped, I hoped, I hoped.

I held out my hands to her now, beckoning her to come to me. She rose from where she'd perched herself on the edge of my aunt's couch, came forward quietly, took my hands, gazing into my eyes with no reservation, no wavering, head held high.

"Welcome," I whispered, and then felt the familiar embarrassment when someone new came to a ritual. It was all very dramatic, and I guess if you came to it without an open mind, or with a sarcastic bent, it might seem very silly. But her eyes were wide and wondering, and I didn't think she'd make fun of me, no matter what happened. I drew her into the room, and together, we stood on either side of the coffee table.

"Um," I said eloquently, still holding her hands, now forming a circle between us. "Do you want me to explain the stuff on the altar? Do you want me to explain what I'm doing..." I cleared my throat, swallowed. "What do you need from me?" I asked then, simply.

She shook her head, squeezed my hands. "I need you to do whatever you need to do. I need you to enjoy yourself."

What I really needed in that moment was to pinch myself. Was she real? Was this real? I closed my hands, felt my connection to her, through and over my skin, through and over her skin, hands held, completing a circle.

"Okay," I whispered. "Okay..."

The ritual began.

"We have come here, you and I, to celebrate the fullness of the moon," I whispered quietly, drawing back the curtains, letting the full moonlight wash into the room. "We celebrate her bounty and her beauty. We recognize that the waning year is here. We know that Samhain is coming..."

Morgan watched me curiously, eyes never wavering from my face as I invoked the moonlight, the four elements in succession, the Goddess into the circle. She watched me spin the magic; she held my hands when I asked her to. She turned deosil—clockwise—when I did, and widdershins—counterclockwise—when I did, and she followed my directives with ease.

When it was all done and over, and we sat across from each other, the full moon candle extinguished, I opened my eyes, felt the energies go out into the world, felt the beauty and love of my Goddess filling every nook and cranny of my home. And Morgan was smiling at me, not a wide smile, but sincere, and I was speechless to see that there were tears in her eyes.

"Um..." I said carefully. "What did you...think?" I squeaked on the last word, and sighed a little.

She held out her arms to me, and when I drew close, she gathered me in, sat me on her lap, embraced me so thoroughly, that, in that single, shining moment, I'd never felt closer to anyone.

"I loved it," she breathed, her face hot against my neck. My heartbeat roared through me as she brushed her warm, soft lips against my skin there. She growled: "Your love for your deity, for the magic...it outshines everything. It was *beautiful*."

I breathed out in a soft sigh, but not from the compliment. The way she held me was warm, close, shiver-causing, as she traced her long, hot fingertips in small circles over the skin of my back, just beneath the hem of my shirt.

"Have you ever," she whispered, kissing my neck, "read *Persuasion*? Jane Austen?"

What? I laughed a little. "Um. No."

"Yay," she said coyly, kissing my collarbone. A thrill raced through me. "You won't think I'm cheesy, then. Ahem."

What was she talking about? I stayed very still as she breathed hotly against my neck, and then her voice in a low growl murmured, *"You pierce my soul."* Her mouth against my neck was now tracing down, and her tongue was against my skin. I shivered against her, my breath coming too quickly now. She continued: *"I am half agony, half hope."* Her hands were up and under my shirt, and she was gripping my hips as she said in her low voice, every word making me shake, *"Tell me not that I am too late..."*

I couldn't breathe, couldn't make a sound as she stilled her hands against me, looked up at me, my heart thundering, beating like a butterfly's wing beneath my skin as she angled up her head, drawing mine down to kiss me.

It was intoxicating, bewitching, beguiling, that kiss, like a spell spun just for me. There were little stars popping along the edges of my vision, and when she slowly lowered me down onto the floor, kneeling over me, I realized: *this is it.* This is happening.

This is now.

And I had never wanted anything more in my entire life than this, right here, right *now*.

Her.

"Persuasion," she growled slowly, carefully, peeling her sweater up and over her head, "is my favorite novel."

"Yeah?" I said weakly, as she pressed

down on me. Her bra was bright blue in the muted candlelight, and when she lowered herself to me to get another kiss, I put my hands up onto her back, tentative and slow, like I was uncertain if I could put them there, if she would mind.

"It's one of the greatest love stories ever told," she whispered into my ear, as I arched beneath her, gasping out as she deftly undid the top button of my jeans. "Do you know why it's so great?" she asked me, her eyes sparkling.

I shook my head, bit my lip as her fingers sought the zipper, tugging it down.

"It promises that, somehow, somewhere, eventually, you will find the one."

I looked up at her, her eyes wide and over me, green and blazing.

"The one," I repeated, twining my fingers in her hair, mystified.

"You," she said, the single word electric between us. She stopped up my mouth with a kiss, drank me in, devoured me like the wolf she was.

I didn't have time to think; I didn't have time to dwell on what she'd told me, the way she'd told me, hands inching up beneath my shirt, her skin hot against mine. She curled her hand beneath my back, lifted me up to her mouth, and there was an indelicate scrabble on my part to dismiss the bra that still covered her. I think I scratched her back, but then the bra was off, and I touched her, felt her, all at once so hungry, I thought I might die from the want of her.

"Here," she said, word rough, growled, as she peeled off my shirt, as she, too, undid the clasp of my bra, letting the straps flow over my shoulders as I shivered, as her mouth moved over my now bare shoulder, tasting my skin like she was savoring me. She moved over me with such grace, such strength, that when she tugged at my pants, urging them over my hips and down my legs, the want was so obvious that when I hooked my fingers into her belt loops, tugging them down her thighs, she pressed me against the floor, and we were just the two of us, with nothing between us.

I wrapped my legs around her waist, felt the floor press against my shoulder blades when she pressed down on top of me, her thighs pushing against my center, and then her hips found my hips as she ground down against me. Her mouth was against my neck, my shoulder, my breasts as she began a rhythm that my body answered, as our hips pressed together. She rose up a little then, her eyes dark and sparking, as she traced a low, curving line, with hot fingertips, down between my breasts, over my stomach, and down and in one, fluid motion, across the center and into me.

The hiss of my breath, my panting, the sound of my wetness, merged with the soft sizzle of the candles on the mantle and the coffee table. We moved together.

Morgan knew me, knew the lines and curves of me, knew the places that drew from me the sighs, and finally a half groan. There was this great symbiosis that drew and stretched on, time out of time, time that remained, suspended. We wanted and needed one another in perfect concert.

This was beauty in the raw definition of the word, beauty that seemed to fill every part of me, just as she filled me, my body, my heart. She was, in those moments, everything I could have dreamed of, and yet, oh, so much more. Every touch was a brand of fire, marking me as hers, as invisible lines radiated off my skin from where she had caressed me. I was marked by want and need, marked, I knew, by love.

A great shudder wracked me, and I saw stars everywhere, stars in everything, and when I opened my eyes there was roaring, a roaring of energy, of magic, pouring through the universe and through her and in her and in me and everywhere. Everywhere was light and stardust, and my woman of the wolf grinned down at me, mouth toothsome and predatory as she devoured my mouth, too, with her own hot tongue, and I felt love in my heart, love as big as the moon.

And then I turned her over, grinning, too, panting, needing.

The crescent moon shone down, covering us like a blanket as we discovered the worlds of one another.

Chapter 11: The Alien

I woke up and couldn't remember how I'd gotten into bed.

Morgan was pillowed in the crook of my arm, her flaming red hair spread out on the pillow like an ascending fire. The blanket was tucked up and over our breasts, and other than that blanket, we were still utterly naked. How *had* we gotten into bed? The last I remembered, we'd been on the living room floor... I took a deep breath and tried to stop smiling so widely as I turned toward the still-sleeping Morgan. God, she was beautiful when she slept, so effortlessly sprawled there, a strong arm still looped around my waist, under the blankets. We were pressed so tightly against one another, and as I pressed my forehead to hers, as I breathed in the heady scent of her, of spice and the woods and all that was, essentially, Morgan, I heard a little *ahem*.

I glanced down in surprise. And at the foot of the bed sat Winifred, grinning down upon us beatifically.

"You said to give you a slight bit of space for the *evening*, as I recall," she murmured pertly, before I could even open my mouth.

"Out," I sighed, with a single raised eyebrow, pointing to the door, even as I grinned at her and shook my head. Probably from the sound of my voice, Morgan began to stir, taking a deep breath as her eyelashes fluttered. And then she was waking up, stretching, yawning…smiling. She smiled at me muzzily, the full corners of her lips turning up sexily as she turned over, pressing her arm over her eyes.

Winnie sighed and floated through the door, leaving us both blissfully alone.

"Hi," I said, twirling a curl of her hair on my finger. I felt suddenly shy, but she kissed me on my nose, yawned again, rolled out of bed and walked into the bathroom without the least bit of self-consciousness, her muscles rippling under her skin as she prowled into the bathroom and shut the door.

I sometimes forgot that she was a werewolf and had probably been seen naked by everyone in town. In all likelihood, she wasn't remotely self-conscious about these sorts of things.

And, anyway, I thought, sitting up on my elbows as I grinned like an idiot…we *had* just slept together.

I glanced in the mirror over my aunt's dresser and saw my disheveled hair, how my makeup was everywhere, felt how I was seriously and deliciously sore, and *oh my goddess, I slept with the woman of my dreams last night, oh my goddess, oh my goddess…*

I heard the toilet flush in the bathroom, and then the door was opening, and Morgan stood in the doorway of the bathroom, brushing her teeth with toothpaste on her finger. She winked at me and laughed a little before she spat in the sink, rinsed out. Watching her do these practiced, normal, everyday actions was unbearably sexy. I don't know why it was. I mean, admittedly, she was completely naked. But I was drinking in the fact that this was the first time she'd been in that bathroom, the first time I'd seen her brush her teeth. The first morning after. And there was an intimacy that was quickly growing between us. We fit together so easily, she and I. And that was delicious.

After a quick drink of water, she prowled back across the space between us and crawled back into bed and over me, and I had to squeak a little and claim having-to-pee-very-very-much-thank-you before she let me go with a smack on my bottom and the promise that when I came back to bed Things Would Happen.

Which they did.

We "got up" officially at noon.

Which is, of course, when Morgan remembered where she was supposed to be.

62

30

"Oh, my God," she said, leaping out of the bed and scrabbling around on the floor for her underwear. "Ninth Order! Ten o'clock! *Late!*"

I helped her find her clothes, got dressed myself, and we drove in my car very, very fast to the coffeeshop.

Victor glared at both of us, rolling his eyes dramatically. "For the sake of a girl, Morgan," he said, shaking his head and tut-tutting. "For the sake of a girl."

"I'm sorry, Victor," she said contritely, hopping the counter and giving him such a big bear hug, I thought I heard something crack. She picked up her apron and tossed it over her head in a flourish. "I'm in love! Please forgive my occasional forgetfulness when love is on the line." She winked at him.

I'm in love, she'd said.

My heart had just skipped so many beats, I was in danger of having it stop altogether.

Victor rolled his eyes again and sighed, putting his hand to his head and flopping down onto the counter. "Yeah, and because of your forgetfulness, missy, I've made over one hundred lattes alone this morning. Over fifty cappuccinos—"

Morgan surveyed the empty shop, her arms wide. "So where are they now?"

I picked up a *Star Trek* logo-shaped pin and turned it over on my palm.

"*They* were all of those alien people. And their bus leaves at one, so they left before you got here. Of *course*," said Victor wryly. "But..." he said, his smile softening his features. "At least the both of you look happy."

Morgan winked at him as she began to brew espresso.

I wandered toward the restroom, wondering if my makeup was as haphazardly put on as I thought it might be. Hands deep in my jeans pockets, I was almost to the ladies' room before I heard a dull thumping sound. For a moment, I wondered if some teenager was passing the coffee shop on the main drag of Wolf Town with his rock music turned up loud, but then I realized that the sound was a lot closer than the street.

It actually sounded like it was coming from the ladies' room.

I tried the knob on the door, but it was locked. I knocked but heard nothing coming from inside. I almost turned and left when I heard a soft thumping from within again, this time coming a bit faster. A bit more frantic.

"Help?" called a woman's muffled voice. "Help? I'm stuck!" I managed to make out from the other side. I pressed my ear to the door as I heard her frantic voice go up another octave. "The door won't *open!*"

I tried the knob again, putting my shoulder into it, but the door was ancient, tall and made out of metal. It wasn't budging.

"Let me get help! Hang in there!" I called out loudly, then sprinted back to the coffee counter.

"There's a lady locked in the restroom," I said breathlessly. Victor didn't even say a word, only rummaged around in what appeared to be a junk drawer behind the counter and emerged with an old-looking set of keys in his hand.

"Happens all the time, unfortunately. We have a mischievous ghost on the premises who keeps locking people in there," he said, with a raised eyebrow and a sigh.

We all trotted over to the restroom hallway, and after a little cajoling, the key turned the lock, and the offending door was opened.

The woman inside, leaning against the doorframe and looking a little pale, was dressed exactly like Captain Janeway (including a wig). She actually looked strikingly like her, waving her thanks at us but not saying a word as she bolted out the door.

"Oh, *noooo*," she groaned, slumping when she entered the main room of the coffee shop and surveyed the empty tables and chairs. "Where did they all go? Am I too late?"

"You were with the group?" asked Victor, dropping the keys on the counter as he slid behind it.

"No, I always walk around dressed like a *Star Trek* character," she snapped.

"I mean, I'm sure some people do." His smile had sugar in it, but when he opened up his mouth that wide, it was easy to see that his incisors were sharp. "I'm sorry. Your friends left fifteen minutes ago."

"If I don't get to the...the bus stop in time, I'm screwed. You don't even understand," she said, shaking her head, tears springing to the corners of her eyes. She changed from angry to utterly deflated in less than two seconds. "You don't understand," she repeated quietly. "I can never get home..."

"There are always other buses," said Morgan, adding whipped cream to my latte.

"No, no, *no!*" the woman wailed, startling all of us. We gazed at her with wide eyes as she spread her hands, turned to the coffee counter beseechingly. "You don't understand. If I don't get to that bus, there's...there's never going to be another one!"

Victor and Morgan exchanged a pointed glance then, eyes widening and mouths opening, but I shook my head, cleared my throat. "Um...but there are always buses—" I began.

"Can someone drive me there?" she interjected. "Please? I'll pay for the gas, for the time—*anything*! Anything at all! Please..." she said, and my jaw dropped as she began to cry in earnest, face in hands. Something I hadn't exactly expected a Captain Janeway lookalike to do.

"Oh, gosh. I mean, I have a car. I can take you," I offered, holding out my hand to her. She was so distraught, I didn't know what else to do.

"I can go with you! I've never seen one of them take off!" crowed Morgan, leaping the counter and shrugging out of her apron.

"We've wanted to see them take off for *years*," said Victor, already shrugging out of his apron, too, and grabbing the coffeeshop keys off the hook in the back. He let himself out from around the counter at a jog. "But you guys are just ridiculous with your security, and we could never get close enough. I'll close up shop! We'll all go!"

The Janeway-woman shrugged, face beseeching, "Sure, sure, fine, the more the merrier. I don't even care anymore. They weren't supposed to leave unless everyone was with them, so screw the security. Just please help me get there?" she asked, her hands clasped in front of her.

"I'm sorry," I said uncertainly with a small frown. "But, um, we *are* going to a bus station, correct?"

"No. She didn't know that we knew, but we know." Morgan handed me my hoodie from its spot on the chair, and Victor and Morgan trotted through the coffeeshop with me — utterly mystified — at their heels.

Victor switched the sign from "open" to

"closed" in a second, slamming the door shut behind us and locking it.

"What did you mean about *taking off*?" I muttered, as Morgan grabbed my hand and squeezed it with a smile.

"I'll explain on the way, I promise," she said, winking.

Victor, Morgan, the Janeway-look alike and myself all ran to my car, parked in front of the Witch Way Café, as the skies erupted, an autumnal storm drenching the town in a roaring deluge.

This wasn't really how I thought my day was going to go.

"So...you're an alien," I repeated weakly, trying to see through the windshield that was completely pounded by rain, making visibilty next to nothing, even with the windshield wipers going at full blast. My knuckles were white on the wheel. I'd driven in a lot of bad storms (I was a New Englander, after all), but this one kind of took the cake. It was like all of the storms of the year had been saving up their rain for this particular day.

We crawled along the road as the recent conversation swirled in my brain.

"Well, yes, according to your language, I'm an alien," said the Captain Janeway lady, who had assured me her real name was something I couldn't pronounce (since it was in an alien tongue) but that I could call her Anna.

An alien. After lake monsters and werewolves and vampires...sure. I could believe in aliens. Couldn't I?

I glanced at Anna in the rearview mirror and swallowed a little. She didn't look like one of those large-eyed, gray-headed types of aliens that you see on documentaries about Roswell. She looked, in fact, perfectly human.

I cleared my throat. "And you and your kind have been coming to Wolf Town for—"

"About fifty years," she nodded, sitting back in the seat and chewing on her lower lip. "We've been on earth for that long, watching humans, studying you. But our mission is over, and we've been sent a ship to take us back to our world. We've been waiting for that ship to land, and we kept getting the dates mixed up. But we've finally coordinated it," she said proudly. "It's landing outside of Wolf Town..." She glanced down at, I assume, her wristwatch. "Well, it's landing right about now."

"And that's the only way you can get home. To your world," I repeated part of her story back, blinking as I said those strange words.

I was talking to an alien. It was taking a little getting used to.

"Yes," she said, sounding wistful. "We've

been here so long, and if we miss it, the earth's pull and trajectory will make going home impossible for another full year. And, personally, I can't wait that long. I can't wait to go home."

"And your home is…" I let that sentence trail off, glancing at her again in the rearview mirror.

"My home world is called Grok, and is the planet that is located in what your kind call the constellation Orion. It's in his belt!"

I blinked.

A planet in Orion's belt. Right.

The storm refused to let up as we neared the state park that Anna swore, up and down, contained the coordinates for where the spacecraft was supposed to have landed. As we turned onto the main road for the park, the rain actually thickened, something that I hadn't even thought possible. Buckets and buckets of more water poured over my poor Subaru's front window, so much so that the wipers almost gave up, sort of flopping back and forth in an effort to make the road slightly visible. They were failing miserably.

"Don't worry," Morgan told Anna, turning to glance at her in the backseat and pat her arm. "Even if you're a little late, they can't possibly take off in all of this. Can they?"

Anna shook her head, bit her lip, stared out the window. "I'm not so sure about that," she muttered.

I pressed harder on the gas.

There was a slim spit of parking area on the edge of the state park. I sort of beached the car as best I could on the rain-soaked pebbles, and then we all bailed out, up to our ankles in freezing rainwater that was slucing off from the surrounding rock-filled forest. I had no umbrellas or rain gear, so the utterly cold water poured over us as we stumbled through the water and pebbles toward the woods. Anna cast about in frustration.

"We knew it was supposed to land near here, but we were never given clear communications." She glanced at Victor in surprise when he groaned. "In any sort of normal circumstance," she told him curtly, "a spaceship is *awfully* hard to miss."

We waited as Anna glanced around uncertainly—a very human response—and when she picked one of the paths and set off down it, the only decent thing to do was to follow her. So we did.

Under the broad arms of colorful maples and evergreens, the torrential downpour was somewhat lessened. Anna was trotting now ahead of us.

"I think it might be this way!" she called back, voice almost swallowed by the roar of thunder. Morgan reached across the space between us and took my hand in her own warm one, squeezing tightly. We began to pick up the pace.

A bolt of lightning zigged and zagged through the air, striking a tree not fifty feet away. The flash was so brilliant it blinded me for a full few heartbeats.

"This is dangerous!" shouted Morgan over the roar of thunder that followed. "I mean, it's going to be a gigantic metal ship, this spaceship, yes? Won't that draw lightning?"

"Probably. Why is that a problem?" Victor shouted back, peering at her through the downpour.

"Problem?" said Morgan, spluttering rain out of her mouth and mopping her red curls out of her face. "Of course you don't care!" she chided him. "You're a vampire, and I'm a werewolf. But you're forgetting that Amy is human—no offense, sweetie," she told me.

"None taken," I replied mildly.

There was a scream up ahead; it sounded like a woman's scream, short and sharp and cut off pretty quickly. For the limited time that I had known her, I was still able to recognize Anna's voice. Anna had made that scream.

We ran toward the source of the sound, stumbling through the torrential downpour, running into branches... Well, that was probably only *me* running into branches. When I managed to glance through the rain at Morgan, I realized that she was leaping effortlessly past the trees as easily as if she were already in wolf form.

We got through the woods and came out pretty suddenly (it was really, *really* hard to see) onto an open field. The rain poured around us in solid sheets of water, but there ahead of us was a dark, writhing shadow in the middle of the meadow. I couldn't make out exactly what it was, but as we got closer, I figured out that it was a group of people milling about in the center of the meadow. The scream that Anna had made was one of excitement, we gathered, as Anna was hugging every single one of the people gathered, crying happily.

The spaceship was nowhere to be seen.

Another crash of lightning, this time along the border of the meadow, arched out of the sky, bringing with it a roll of thunder that was so loud the ground itself shook beneath our feet. The spear of lightning connected to a tree on the edge of the meadow: one of the tallest trees shattered in two, one particularly large, claw-like branch falling off in a low groan as it toppled to the ground.

"This lightning is all part of the landing procedure, because of the electric currents of the ship!" yelled Anna over the noise of the thunder to us. "Don't worry. It's all right! We're perfectly safe here!"

It's not that I didn't want to believe her, but it was hard not to be doubtful as the intensity of the lightning picked up, bolts beginning to hit trees surrounding the meadow at an alarmingly faster rate. There was a constant roll of thunder around us now, the earth beneath our feet shaking.

Morgan put her arm about my shoulder, and I shivered — partly because of the cold, partly because of the massive amounts of lightning raining down around us, and partly because of how her warmth instantly made me feel: loved. There was such a closeness now between us, a fresh, new joy that flooded me each time I looked at her, watched her flashing green eyes take me in like I was the only thing in the world that mattered.

It was an odd circumstance to have this thought in, granted, but it wholly consumed me in that heartbeat. I knew that my heart belonged to her. Only to her, forever.

I threaded my fingers through hers and squeezed her hand. I could see her smile in the rain, her mouth turning sexily up at the corners, even in this cold, torrential downpour. She ducked forward a little, moving as fast as a wolf on the hunt, and pressed her hot mouth against the side of my face and my nose, her smile turning into a full grin as she glanced away then, squeezing my hand even tighter.

As I felt the blush rise in my cheeks (and other parts of me turning extremely hot), I knew that I could totally face a freezing October thunderstorm: I had love on my side!

I wondered fleetingly if people who died of pneumonia had ever had such steadfast convictions that love would keep them warm and dry.

Nah...

"It's coming!" Cries broke out around us, and some cheering. "It's *here!*"

We peered up, shielding our eyes from the rain. We didn't see anything but more storm clouds and lightning arcing through them at a dizzying pace. I kept peering up, shielding my eyes from the rain as best as I was able to, and in a moment, the rain began to lessen until it was only a few fat drops falling down around us to absolutely nothing. The clouds were dark and menacing, but the stormhad gone from a complete downpour to not raining at all — almost as quickly as if someone had turned off the tap.

And out of the clouds...it arrived.

The spaceship (because that's really all it could possibly have been) was round and enormous, a shining silver oblong object that flashed in the lightning that began to hit the earth around us. But it wasn't the usual lightning — that mostly kills you on the spot. The bolts didn't hit like they might destroy trees and humans but as if they were fingers of a god, caressing the dirt. The arcs of lightning lingered, staying for half a minute, a minute, suspended from the earth to the surface of the spaceship.

Sort of as if the lightning was holding the spaceship up. And it was now lowering the spaceship down.

The ship landed silently, effortlessly, like someone had thrown down a giant's pillow from the clouds. It hovered for a heartbeat about five feet above the ground, rotating in space, and long, spider-like metallic limbs disengaged from the hull, touching the ground and finally settling.

A door in the side opened without sound, lowering to the ground like a ramp. White lights were flashing on and off inside.

We all stared at it, our mouths open. At least, the vampire and the werewolf and myself, the witch, were staring at it with our mouths open. The aliens stared at it with longing, and with joy.

"This is goodbye!" said Anna joyously, turning quickly and hugging each one of us, one after the other. She pressed her purse to me with a smile. "Please keep whatever is in here for the trouble of driving me all the way out here. I appreciate it so much!" she said. Tearfully, she turned and almost ran up the ramp, followed by several people from *Star Trek*, moonwalkers and a Wookie or two. Anna's *Star Trek* uniform looked especially striking ascending a real-life *alien spaceship*.

I still hadn't been able to shut my mouth.

Calmly, the people formed one long line

and marched into the spaceship. When all were inside, as effortlessly as it had landed, the silver spaceship sucked in its thin legs, hovered for a heartbeat, and glided off and up, through the stormclouds, the lightning seemingly lifting it into the air. The spaceship parted the clouds, and then the dark clouds had swallowed it completely.

And it was gone.

The three of us stared for a long moment; then we glanced at one another with wide eyes.

Victor crossed his arms, looking up, working his jaw. "Well," he said, drawing out the word with a slight eyeroll, "that was certainly a lot less theatrical than Spielberg would have led me to believe," he said, after a long moment. "But still nice. That landing was a pure ten." He wrinkled his nose. "The takeoff could have been better."

"Aliens," I managed, and I could hear the awe in my voice.

"Are you kidding me? You've been witness to werewolves, vampires and lake monsters since you got to town," Victor snorted. "Aliens should sort of be expected at this point."

We all stared up at the sky for a moment longer.

"True," I said, biting my lip.

"We're going to catch our death. Except for maybe the vampire," Morgan quipped, tugging my hand and drawing me against her warm body and wrapping her arms around me tightly. "Let's head back and get some warm dinner," she murmured in a low growl into my ear.

"Oh, damn it, I should have taken a pic with my cell phone," Victor muttered, drawing his smartphone (his slightly *damp* smartphone) out of a coat pocket and thumbing it with a frown.

Morgan chuckled and placed her arm around my shoulder, and together, the three of us turned to head back toward the car. And as we walked together through the dripping, quiet woods, I realized that my life had gotten interesting in all sorts of unexpected ways, and that I wouldn't trade it for anything.

Back in the meadow, on the ground, lay a drenched headband with sparkly alien antennae.

Chapter 12: The Invitation

They say that an alien encounter can bring people together. I just think Victor wanted a dinner that he didn't have to cook. Either way, we somehow ended up at the door to the Witch Way Café as I fumbled with the keys and let all three of us into the quiet, empty space.

Victor stood in the doorway, nose wrinkled, as he glanced into the café.

"What?" I asked, throwing my arms wide. "Don't you like the redecorating job?"

"No, it's not that," he sighed, pinching the bridge of my nose. "But I can't come in. You have to invite me."

"What?" I asked, not understanding.

"I'm a vampire," he said slowly (and a bit patronizingly). "You have to invite me in, or I can't *come* in."

I stared at him, blinking. "My aunt never invited you into the café?"

He frowned a little, one eyebrow raised. "She found me..." He pursed his lips. "Well..."

"Your aunt was a little racist toward vampires," said Morgan gently, brushing past me into the café and depositing her sopping wet coat on the coatrack, placing her hands on her hips and smiling encouragingly at me.

"So..." I trailed off. I curled my finger towards him.

"You can just say 'c'mere,' like I'm some sort of highly trained puppy," he told me, rolling his eyes.

I chuckled at that. "Come here, then, vampire. How is that *any* better?"

"It's not," he told me imperiously, stalking into the café and kicking out one of the chairs and sitting in it backwards, like he was about to star in a boy band music video from the nineties. "What do you serve in this joint?"

I chuckled at him and grabbed one of the laminated menus from the cash register. "It's your awesome, standard diner food. What'll you have to drink?" I asked him, taking one of the aprons off the hook behind the register and placing it over my head.

He sighed and didn't even glance at the menu before tossing it onto the tabletop. "I'll take a plate of eggs, bacon and wheat toast," he said with a small yawn.

"And for you?" I asked, my heart beating a little bit faster when I glanced in the direction of Morgan. I just *glanced* in her direction, and already my heart was beating so quickly against my ribs that I had to take a deep breath.

"Just tea," she said, with a small sideways smile, and sat down gracefully next to Victor at the diner table.

"You got it," I told them, lighting the burner on the stove in the kitchen. It wasn't really so much a kitchen as an area behind the cash register that included burners and counterspace. I dragged the bacon and eggs out of the walk-in fridge and began to prepare the meal. I also put the kettle on.

"I still can't believe vampires eat," I said with raised eyebrows as I threw bacon onto a frying pan.

"We should do a show and tell!" said Victor blithely, leaning forward against the chair and smiling toothily at me. "The differences between vampires and werewolves—it'd be most informative. And, anyway, you'll want to know all of this to be politically correct in Wolf Town."

"Politically correct in Wolf Town," I repeated with a chuckle, turning the bacon on the pan as it began to sizzle. "There's a sentence you don't hear every day."

As I worked at the stove, Winnie wandered down the steps from the upstairs apartment, her nose wrinkled. She floated about a foot above the steps, and she had a ghostly book in her hands, which she promptly dropped once she'd spotted Victor. Well, the book didn't so much drop as float in mid-air. Her eyebrows furrowed as she stared the vampire down. "What's *he* doing here?" she huffed, crossing her arms. "Seriously, Amy, vampires aren't the nicest sorts of people—"

"I can hear you, you know," said Victor, looking directly at her. "God, you even have a ghost problem in this joint."

"Ghosts?" said Morgan, raising an eyebrow. "Amy, you have ghosts?"

"Just one, and she's very friendly," I said, smiling encouragingly as I placed a few slices of wheat bread in the toaster. "Winnie, please be nice. And, Victor, I can uninvite you, you know."

"You can't!" he said blithely. "It's in the rules."

Winnie sighed out and hovered above one of the steps with a small frown. "He's right," she muttered. Then: "I'm going back up. Tell me when *he's* gone," she said with a frown, drifting back up toward the apartment, and presumably through the door and out of sight.

"How *did* you end up in Wolf Town, Victor?" I asked. I began cracking eggs.

Morgan chuckled at that, running her long fingers through her still-damp red hair. It was beginning to dry, the humidity and the rain making it curl in every direction. "It's because Victor's weird, and he had this uncanny ability to find us other weirdos," she said with a dry laugh.

"That's true. Sort of," he agreed with another toothy grin. "I came over to the states from Europe about a hundred years ago, actually. I was originally from... I guess it used to the Czech Republic, but I have no clue what it is now. I haven't really kept up with family affairs," he shrugged. "Anyway, I wasn't a *grand, rich* vampire, by any stretch of the imagination, and I wanted to start over in America. I knew about Wolf Town because I knew a few werewolves that were part of the MacRue clan over there." He jerked his thumb in the presumed direction of Europe. "They said it was a great place to lay down stakes. As it were..." He laughed at his own joke. Both Morgan and I groaned.

I scooped the bacon, eggs and toast onto a plate, artfully arranging a few packets of butter around the toast and waltzing it over to their table. I set it down in front of him, and he smiled appreciatively down at his plate, tucking a napkin over his lap. I sat down next to him, flipping the spatula in my hands as I waited for the tea kettle to whistle. "I hope you like it," I told him as he tucked in.

"Oh, gods, it's heavenly," he said inarticulately around a massive mouthful of egg. "It wouldn't be better if there was blood on it. Well, maybe a little," he amended, seamlessly transitioning to that thought as I grimaced. "Oh! Before I forget," said Victor, tapping the table in front of Morgan. "You, missy — the Blood Dance is this Wednesday."

The werewolf sighed and slumped forward in her chair. I glanced from one to the other and shook my head. "Blood Dance?" I asked.

"Well, you see, there are actually quite a few vampires in Moon Run," said Victor around a mouthful of crunchy toast. "We always make an appearance at the Wolf Town Hallow's Eve Fair and masquerade every year, but we put on a dance of our own two days before the Fair. Vampires have to be first," he sniffed. "It's, like, a *thing*. And, traditionally, Morgan has always been my buddy date." He sighed long-sufferingly. "I can't believe I just said that."

"I'm your buddy!" Morgan crowed. "Oh, that must be so painful to you..."

"So, you can't have her for that one night," said Victor then, dabbing at the corners of his mouth with his napkin. "Sorry about that. It's not like I *want* a buddy date," he sighed, raising his eyes to the heavens, "but I seem to be on a date shortage lately."

"Well, I hope that shortage clears up soon?" I said uncertainly, then sighed and glanced at Morgan. "And I suppose I can get along without her for one night..." I gave her a wistful look, though. I mean, I *would* miss her. I was falling in love with her. But I was sure I could find some mischief to get up to on my own...

My phone rang, filling the air with the

tinny sounds of Tchaikovsky and startling all of us—including Winnie, who jumped just a little (she was currently floating at the very top of the stairs. She was apparently too interested in our conversation to sequester herself away).

"Sorry, I have to take this..." I muttered when I glanced down at the screen and saw who it was. I got up, trotted quickly to the front door and let myself out into the night. "Hello... Mom?" I said warmly.

"Hi, sweetheart!" she crowed through the receiver. "How is my baby girl?"

"Fabulous!" I smiled, tucking a strand of hair behind my ear as I glanced down at my shoes and put my other hand into my jeans pockets. "Like, really, really good, Mom," I told her then, hearing the glow in my words.

"Oh, sweetheart, that's wonderful," she said, and on the other end of the phone, I could hear the door to the oven opening and shutting, and what sounded like a tray being set on the counter. Of *course* she was multi-tasking while talking to me. "Can we talk about your love muffin?" she asked then.

I chuckled so hard that I had to stop to catch my breath. "Love muffin? Oh, Mom," I said with another chuckle. "I'd love to, really," I told her, glancing up at the still-threatening stormclouds hanging over Wolf Town, "but I have company over right now—"

"Say no more, sweetheart. I won't keep

you, then! But the girls and I were talking, and we were thinking that we all might make the trip up to Wolf Town for Samhain weekend! We wanted to see the café, and isn't that when Bette is supposed to be getting back into town?"

"Um," I began, but I was cut off.

"And we could see how you were getting on... And celebrate Samhain, of course! Isn't that a wonderful idea?"

I swallowed, glancing backward into the café and to Morgan, who was chuckling at something that Victor had said. Seeing my mom again would be wonderful, obviously — but, I mean — the whole *coven*?

Morgan was a werewolf, sure. But she'd never faced an entire coven of witches before.

"Sure!" I said weakly. "That'll be fun! But, Mom," I said then, raising an eyebrow, "are you just totally bringing all of the ladies up to judge Morgan? To see if she's good material for your one and only daughter?"

"You see right through me, sweetheart," she said, without a touch of guilt. Which meant that, yes, absolutely, that was a major reason for her trip. "So, that's wonderful. I'm so glad that we could discuss this!" she sang into the phone. "We'll come up Thursday night!"

"I can't wait to see you guys," I told her sincerely. "And you'll probably love it. There's supposed to be a big carnival and all sorts of fun stuff," I told her, glancing back into the café again. Morgan and Victor's heads were bent together as they discussed something serious.

"I'll call you later!" said my mom, and—making some smooching sounds—she hung up.

I smiled as I pocketed my phone and went back into the café, the door's bells ringing behind me as I shut it.

"So," I began, but Morgan glanced at me with a sly smile and held up her hand.

"I heard it all," she said, then looked a little penitent. "Sorry, a wolf has very good hearing," she said, tapping her right ear and straightening in her seat. "I'd love to meet your mom," she said, completely sincere as she gazed up at me.

I leaned against the wall, folding my arms as I winced. "That's very sweet of you," I said then, trying to find the words with which to prepare her for this coming weekend. "But my mom is going to be bringing her entourage. Are you sure you want to meet all of them? I mean, they get kind of crazy..."

Victor and Morgan exchanged a glance, the vampire throwing up his hands to encompass, I assume, the entire town.

"It's Wolf Town," he said, with a shake of his head. "We deal in weird like it's our own currency."

"True," I said with a small smile. I sat down next to them again, indicated Victor's empty plate. "Good?"

"Almost as good as blood," he promised, tossing his napkin onto the empty plate.

I...suppose that was a compliment.

Chapter 13: The Lake Monster

I made myself a cup of tea and waited for Morgan on the front steps of the shop, wrapped up in my sweater, the late afternoon sunshine washing the entire main street of the town in gold.

The many dirty dishes would wait until early tomorrow morning; I hadn't realized how busy the café could get, since there weren't that many people in the town to begin with, but, my goodness, the café had been crowded today. The tables were full until after I'd closed. Is this what I should expect every day?

I watched the leaves of the oak in front of the Café drift down, teased off the branches with a fine wind. There was so much possibility in the air, in the wind, in the leaves and the steam that curled up like spirals from my teacup. I was exhausted, but it was a good kind of exhausted; I'd made my aunt a lot of profit with tasty diner food that put smiles on people's faces.

It'd been a tiring but good day.

Morgan came up the street, her long red coat open, hands buried deep in pockets and her beautiful, strong face bent toward the ground, as if she were deep in thought. But as she approached me, I saw her nose begin to twitch, and then she glanced up. When she saw me, the smile that lit up her face was astronomical in its span, and when she came close, she offered her hands to me; she helped me up and into her warm embrace and kiss and hello.

She tasted like coffee and spices, and her mouth was as warm and inviting and lovely as she was.

I was waiting for cartoon hearts to start appearing around us, accompanied by an extremely sappy love song pumped through some invisible speakers, but the moment didn't last. We broke apart as Burt neared us, stalking down the sidewalk in an extreme hurry, face cast in a downward-swooping frown.

"Oh, no," said Morgan the moment she saw him, raising her brows to the heavens. "Burt, what's wrong?"

"Something terrible, I'm afraid, Morgan." He shook his head. "It's the water pipes *again*. I really need to talk to your father about this, about what's happening with the town and its safeguards. They don't appear to be functioning at *all*, at this point."

"There's another break in the pipes?" I asked Burt, eyes wide as I tightened my grip on Morgan's right hip, fingers curling reflexively as I thought about the creature that had tried to attack us in the abandoned factory. "I thought the mermaid left," I told him.

"I think that the mermaid was only *part* of the problem, unfortunately—not the *entire* problem," said Burt, looking miserable as he kind of sagged there, standing on the sidewalk and leaning back on his heels, like he wanted to declare "uncle" to the universe. "I'm not certain *what* it could be this time. But there are a few breaks in the pipes, and we have to turn off the water again, Amy. I'm sorry about that."

"I wanted to wait to do dishes until tomorrow, anyway," I assured him with a smile. "Don't even worry about it."

"Burt, we really need to get to the bottom of this," said Morgan, voice low, hackles raised as she bit off the last word with a growl, her lips over her teeth. "This is getting ridiculous," she snapped. "After we find out what's wrong," she said, nodding to Burt, "I'm going to talk to my father about it again. He wasn't very helpful when I brought it up with him last time. Have you gotten a chance to talk to him about it?"

Burt shook his head. "He said he's been in too many meetings."

Morgan stared at the man, her eyes narrowing. "Really? That's odd..." she muttered.

"But, yes, if you want to help, be my guest. I could really use the help. I'm kind of at my wit's end. Do you ladies want to come to the plant with me and look at the old break? Maybe it's broken through again, and maybe this time we can find, once and for all, the root of this problem and fix it." He sighed. Burt looked more haggard than he ever had before, haggard and defeated.

I looked about, at the sun setting, at the encroaching darkness. Going to an abandoned factory that may or may not contain a monster, and so close to Samhain, wasn't really my idea of fun. But he *did* look desperate, and he was such a good guy. I couldn't imagine dealing with this problem by myself, and so far, that's exactly what he'd had to do.

"I'll go with you guys," I offered with a small smile. "It's okay, Burt," I told him, zipping up my hoodie as we turned and together walked down the sidewalk in the direction of the outskirts of town and the abandoned factory. "Try to think positively?" I suggested, with a grimace, and then another small, encouraging smile. "It's *probably* not another killer mermaid, right?" I joked. And then I realized that was a *terrible* joke.

"It could be *anything*, including another killer mermaid," said Burt with a groan, taking off his glasses and rubbing at his eyes with a tired hand. "Anything in the whole damn mystical ocean, deciding to flop upstream, using *our* pipes to do it in!"

I bit my lip and trotted after the both of them as darkness descended over Wolf Town like the beginning of a nightmare.

"You know," I said, as Morgan struck a match, lighting the candle in the old-fashioned lantern, "if you could have told me a few months ago that I'd be searching through an abandoned shoe factory with a werewolf, looking for a possible sea monster in some water pipes, I would have thought you were slightly crazy. Or a writer. Which is sometimes the same thing," I pointed out, as she shut the lantern door. It was warm to the touch already from the small flame.

She shot me a half-smile in the guttering candlelight. "Well," she said softly, reaching across the space between us to take my hand, "I'm glad you're here."

Burt's flashlight had been out of batteries, so he'd remembered there had been a few lanterns in the broken-down shed behind the factory. Now, together, we walked into the abandoned factory with only the light of the lantern to guide us. This wasn't ridiculously terrifying at *all*, walking into an abandoned building at twilight with only a guttering lantern and a werewolf between whatever monster had decided to mess up the flow of water again and us. But I trusted Morgan, and, anyway, I'd picked up another big stick outside of the building, and Burt was brandishing his pen. Plus, I'd spun an energetical shield around the three of us as best I could.

We would probably be okay.

Probably.

We moved through the abandoned factory at a snail's pace. Morgan walked through it a little more confidently than the rest of us, thanks to her wolfish qualities, but it was almost too dark to see anything other than the nightmarish structure of the factory, which thoroughly creeped me out. I remembered that there was a gigantic hole in the floor, and I wanted to avoid falling into it...

But there it was, in the center of the room, clearly visible by the lantern's light. Morgan crept up to the edge of that hole and peered down and in, her brows furrowed.

"Welp. That's odd. It's still fixed. The water's flowing through completely undisturbed," she announced, lowering the lantern a little. "There's nothing down there."

Of course, a tentacle chose that exact instant to come up and over the lip of the hole and wrap itself around her legs. It was like a very bad horror movie; the tentacle had suction cups, and looked, for all intents and purposes, like a gigantic octopus arm.

Morgan glanced down at the tentacle wrapped around her legs, sighed, set the lantern down on the ground and with effortless grace stepped out of the loops of the tentacle. "Really?" she asked sharply, glaring down into the hole.

The tentacle sheepishly sank back down into the hole.

"It's one of Ellie's kids," she said, crouching at the edge and lifting the lantern up and then down into the hole. "Aw, c'mon, little guy..."

There was a hiss, much louder (and, admittedly, much scarier) than a cat's.

Burt and I came to the edge, too, mystified.

The baby, if something that large could be *called* a baby, didn't look much like Ellie, though it did have a long neck and a horse-shaped head. Instead of flippers, it had about six tentacles at varying lengths around the edge of its oddly shaped body. The body reminded me a little of a pool floaty. The creature crouched in a corner of the level below us, down in the hole. It had its head lowered, sharp teeth bared, hissing very slowly at the three of us, like a tire with a slow leak.

"Okay, so where did it come from, if there isn't a break?" I pointed to the solid pipes.

"Maybe farther down the pipes. Either way, I think they're trying to sneak from Wolf Town out to the ocean again," said Morgan, shaking her head. "I mean, I can understand it. They're wild creatures. Ellie loves Henry, but her kids have no such feelings and want to be free."

"Understandable to want to be free," agreed Burt. "But how do we move her now?"

We were at a loss for a long moment, until we saw her glide across the floor as effortlessly as if she were on wheels, tentacling (is that even a word?) after a rat. She pounced on it, devouring it in one nasty little gulp, tongue flicking over her pin-sharp teeth. She was about the size of a small pony. Which gave me an idea.

"Is...is she friendly? Did Henry raise her? If Henry raised her...I mean, can she be, well, ridden?"

"*Ridden*?" Morgan snorted. "You want to ride a lake monster?"

"Not me," I said, waving my hands. "But if you want to..."

"Oh, nice," she laughed, grinning. "Volunteer the werewolf. Everyone always volunteers the werewolf."

"So, is that a yes?" I asked with a small smile.

She glanced down into the hole with her brows raised. "I don't think I'm going to become a rodeo champion anytime soon. Sorry, but I'm going to have to sit this one out."

The three of us looked down into the hole.

"Any other ideas?" asked Burt weakly.

"Well..." I began, as my cell phone went

off. It was the ringtone I used for my mother, *Toccatta in Fugue*.

All of a sudden, the little beastie's head swung up as quickly as if a string had been pulled. She (for whatever reason, she struck me as female) cocked her head; then slowly — frighteningly, like the stuff of nightmares — she began to climb up the vertical wall toward us, her little tentacles flailing, her suction cups keeping her stuck to the wall as she inched ever forward.

She came up and over the edge of the hole in the floor even as we backed away. Her equine head was down, her big eyes blinking slowly, and her long lashes fluttering. This close, with the lantern flickering, she looked less frightening, though still strange. At least she was no longer hissing.

My cell phone chose that exact moment to stop ringing, and she paused, too, as if surprised, her head up, eyes blinking slowly.

But my mother is a very persistent lady.

The phone began to ring again.

Again, the creature began to tentacle toward me, albeit a little slowly.

All three of us looked to each other.

"So, I think we have a plan, then?" asked Morgan, her arms crossed.

"Well," I said, holding up my hot pink phone. "It's better than creating a lake monster rodeo, admittedly."

My mother was persistent, but she wasn't more persistent than a couple of phone calls. I dialed up a browser on my phone and then played a video of a tinny version of the song. It was about a mile to Henry's house. That song was never going to get out of my head, but as we walked slowly out of the factory and toward the broken sidewalk on the edge of town, the strange creature followed us with a docile, calm expression, occasionally snapping at a moth that fluttered too close to the lantern.

"We're officially lake monster wranglers," said Morgan with a chuckle, wrapping her arm around my waist as we walked together.

"I'll make sure to put that on my resumé," I chuckled.

We moved through the well-lit streets of Wolf Town, all the way to Henry's place. All of the lights were on in Henry's impressive household, causing it to light up like a beacon on the edge of the small lake/pond/monster-home behind the house.

Henry had obviously realized that one of his pet's babies was missing, because he was sitting on his porch, his arms folded and his foot tapping nervously. When he saw us, he leapt up and bolted down the steps, quite quickly for an older gentleman.

"Oh, my goodness, Sasha!" Henry exclaimed, trotting past us, right up to the little monster that towered over him but was still subjected to a very big squeeze, the man tenderly placing his arms about the beast's neck.

"I was so worried about you!" Henry said, and when he stepped back, it looked as if he had tears in his eyes. He wiped them away with a sigh, shaking his head. "I hope you know that you are in *so* much trouble..." Henry began as the beastie, Sasha, lowered her head, batting her long-lashed eyes at him in what I presumed to be some semblance of being sorry. "Go home!" intoned Henry, pointing down to the lake, where Ellie splashed about in the shallows anxiously.

Ellie had about ten offspring in various sizes of hugeness cavorting around her. I blinked, watched them swim around their mother. Some of them were almost as big as she was.

"So, so, so sorry about that," said Henry, deflating as Sasha slithered into the lake.

"This can't keep happening," said Burt, shaking his head. "I'm sorry, Henry, but this just *can't* keep happening."

"I can't think of a solution," he said, spreading his hands. "I wish I could. I'm doing everything I can. I built the fence. I stopped up the drains... They keep finding fun and exciting ways to escape." He sighed, rubbed at his eyes; he looked exhausted. "You just don't know what it's like. They're trying to *kill* me with worry! What I don't understand," he said, after a long moment, "is how they're even able to get out. The town is supposed to help prevent that. There are safeguards everywhere, but their stopping up the drains should trigger the safeguard from Wolf Town itself. They shouldn't be able to get out if the safeguard is still in place. It *is* in place, right, Morgan?" He exchanged a glance with Morgan. She shrugged uncomfortably.

"I'm sure it is, Henry," she said. I stared at her in surprise.

I knew, in that moment, that she was lying. She wasn't sure it was. She wasn't sure at all.

I watched Sasha slip into the water, watched her big momma bite her neck, shake her a little like a mother dog might scold a very naughty puppy. It was kind of sweet, if you took the tentacles and gigantic teeth out of the picture.

"So, our work here is done!" I said, valiantly and with slight exhaustion. An incredibly busy morning and afternoon at the café, and then playing dog catcher for a monster: I'd had a big day.

Burt sighed. "We have to come up with a solution for this," he said in frustration, with a shake of his head.

"I can make some tea?" offered Henry. "We can sip it on the back porch, watch the kids like hawks and make sure they don't get out while we discuss ideas."

"Sounds great," I muttered, climbing the steps to his veranda and sprawling on the cushioned rocker. It swung back and forth. I buried my hands deep into my hoodie's pockets, doing my absolute best to bite down the edges of crankiness that were beginning to sneak into my voice. I just wanted a warm bath and a warm bed—and a warm Morgan *in* said bed. I was not looking forward to the dishes in the morning.

Morgan sat down beside me on the swing, and I pillowed my head on her shoulder. She wrapped an arm tightly around my shoulders and sighed as she rested her chin on the top of my head. Burt came up and sat on one of the chairs, and eventually Henry came out of the house, the door shutting behind him as he balanced a steaming tea pot and a few mugs overturned on a tray.

In the darkness, I heard vast amounts of splashing, occasional hisses and teeth chomping from down at the pond.

"Ah, my night's symphony," said Henry, giving me a small wink. He seemed to be in a much better mood than the first time I'd met him, despite having his pet's kids escape. I smiled in spite of myself.

"They can't keep messing up the entire water system of Wolf Town, Henry," said Burt clearly, slapping his knees as if he'd prepared a speech. He sat on the edge of his seat and had his hands in front of him, using them for large, sweeping gestures. "It's just not right. It's costing thousands in repairs, and —"

Henry sighed, held his empty mug with two hands. "I think that, first thing tomorrow, I'm going to go have a talk with Mr. MacRue, see if there's something we can do about the safeguards growing weaker," he said quietly. He lifted his head, caught Morgan's eyes. "You do agree that they're weakening, don't you?"

She held that gaze for a long moment, then glanced away. "I'm not certain," she said quietly. "But you're right, Henry. We need to talk to my father. This is all getting out of hand, and if the safeguards are not weakening, then maybe we can discuss with him about what to do with Ellie's kids. But after the Halloween festivities, all right?" she asked, leaning forward a little. "My father has been, well, stressed out because of all of the planning for the carnival and everything," she said, working her jaw. "Does that sound all right with you?"

Henry and Burt exchanged a glance but nodded.

I squeezed Morgan's hand, and she squeezed it back, but she was distracted as she took a long drink of her tea, gazing out to the dark pond.

Overhead, one star shone in the darkness, the first of the night. But I was too tired to even think of making a wish.

Chapter 14: The Dance

My mother was going to arrive tomorrow night—Thursday night—and the Hallow's Eve fair opened Friday night. I sighed and stared at my calendar, poking it.

Morgan and Victor were going to that vampire dance this evening. Morgan had told me she couldn't get out of it, and, anyway, if she didn't go, Victor would have to go all alone, and that would "wound his dignity and ego." I had reminded her that I was completely fine with it, and that she should go and have fun with her friends. I had eleven billion things to do, anyway, in preparation for my mother's arrival. And the coven's arrival. And Samhain...

And then she'd asked me if I was a little overwhelmed with everything, and I'd asked her what she could possibly mean by that, and she told me I'd scrubbed that same clean table five times in the past five minutes.

So I'd admitted a night off might be nice, too. I could spend the entire time in the tub reading if I wanted to—which was mostly my plan.

There was a marked chill in the air

tonight, and I could see my breath beneath the streetlights as I ducked my head out of the café and looked down the sidewalk. I shut and locked the door and turned the "open" sign to "closed." Outside the front door window, the moon was slowly waning and dipped low in the sky, dragging us ever onward through the wheel of the year, toward Samhain.

Samhain. I ran my fingers through my hair, sighed and leaned against the doorjamb. It was almost Samhain. Halloween.

Had I only been in Wolf Town a few short weeks? Sometimes, it seemed like I'd always been here, and, indeed, maybe part of my heart *had* always been tied to this place. I knew it was no coincidence that I was here, knew that there had been a reason for my vision, knew the town had summoned me here on purpose, *for* a purpose.

Part of me believed, wholeheartedly, that the reason I'd been drawn here was for Morgan. Morgan and I were meant to be together, I knew, but, strangely, when I thought about Wolf Town bringing me here, that single explanation didn't feel quite right.

There was another reason I was in Wolf Town.

But whatever the reason was, I felt secure in the knowledge that I was in the right place; it was the right time, almost Samhain, and magic was alive in the world.

I made my weary way up the steps into my aunt's apartment. A postcard from her had arrived in the mail today, and it was sitting on the kitchen table. She expected to be home in early November, and then we'd discuss what had been happening in the café, and she said she'd pay me handsomely for my time here—which felt wrong, since I'd *offered* to help her. I guess most people can't just pick up their lives and help their aunt out for a month, but I was "lucky" enough to be able to do that. Lucky in the fact, of course, that there had been nothing tying me to my old way of life.

I wasn't sure how I felt about my aunt returning. Would I stay in Wolf Town? What kind of job could I get here?

And if I *couldn't* stay in Wolf Town—well, my heart hurt imagining the idea of a long-distance relationship with the woman who occupied my heart. It would be too painful. But what if we had to live and love like that, miles and miles apart?

All of those questions loomed on the horizon, but they were not present in the quiet apartment now, in the quiet bathroom, and I didn't have to think about them. All I had to do was relax.

I drew a bath, and I poured in a liberal amount of bubble-making mixture. The bubbles mounded up like some sort of bubble-monster in a horror movie, but I threw off my clothes and

227

stepped into the water.

And I lay there, and I thought of absolutely nothing. Sometimes, thoughts came to me like clouds scuttling across a mostly blue sky, but—for the most part—my mind was as blank as a plowed-under field, likes the ones lining the forest around Wolf Town.

I thought about absolutely nothing, that is, until Allen MacRue, for whatever reason, appeared in my head. I thought about how strange he'd always behaved toward me...

I thought about the fairies and their demand that I take that letter to him.

I wondered what the letter contained.

Yes, it seemed like it'd been forever since I arrived in Wolf Town, but in some ways, it seemed like I'd gotten here yesterday, because there was so much that I still didn't know about the town itself, and so much about the place that still surprised me every single day. I would probably learn all of Wolf Town's quirks in time, but if there was something nefarious going on, I needed to know about it now. Especially with Samhain so close. Samhain, when the veil between worlds became thin...

Samhain in Wolf Town, I imagined, would likely be the strangest Samhain I'd ever experienced.

I closed my eyes, sighed, covered my face with my hands.

Had I been working too hard? Had this

all of this happened too quickly? Had I been drinking too many caffeinated beverages?

My mind looped in tired, dull circles, and, despite my best intentions, I fell asleep in the bubble-full bathtub.

I woke up when I heard keys at the apartment door, heard Morgan enter the apartment and deposit her bag on the couch. The little cat clock I kept in the bathroom showed two o'clock. I could only assume it was morning and not afternoon, and that I hadn't fallen asleep for days like Rip Van Winkle.

"Hi!" I called, hearing how croaky my voice was. I cleared it, tried again: "I'm in the bath! I'll be out in a minute!"

I was so cold I was shaking; the water had become cool, but, surprisingly, most of the bubbles had remained in the tub—which was crazy, really. I rose out of the bath, grabbed the hanging towel, tried to rub the bubbles off of me.

Winnie and I had a set rule about the bathroom, but Morgan and I had never really talked about such things. She knocked at the door.

"Come in?" I said quietly.

She opened the door.

I let out a huff of breath; suddenly every inch of my skin was vibrating with a shiver, but it wasn't from the cold water anymore. I stared at the jaw-droppingly beautiful woman standing in front of me.

"Um—is that what you wore to the vampire party?" I ventured, after a long moment, feeling suddenly shy.

Morgan wore tight black leather pants and a white ruffled shirt that looked like something someone would have worn at a Shakespeare performance. In her very curly hair, on top of her head, was a mask the color of blood. She'd drawn her hair back into a loose ponytail, and it flowed over her shoulder like fire.

She was breathing a little indelicately and was staring at parts of me I'd covered with a towel, her eyes darkening as her chest rose and fell; fire began to run through me.

I let the towel drop.

When she came forward, when she pressed me back against the cold tiles on the wall in the bath, I could only think two things, really: that she tasted of red wine, and that this was, perhaps, the hottest and most radically unexpected moment of my life. But then that thought kind of got wiped out, along with everything else in the world, when Morgan picked me up with strong arms, still pressing me against the cold tiles of the wall, and I wrapped my legs around her hips.

"Oh, my gods," I hissed, as she pressed her hips hard against mine, grinding herself against my center so hard and with such intensity as she growled against my neck, her teeth and tongue finding my skin there, that all that I was felt that heat surge through me. I wrapped my fingers in her fire-red hair, groaning against her as one arm wrapped around my naked waist and the other gripped my right hip, digging her fingernails into my skin as she pressed me down harder against her hips and right thigh.

I arched against her, moving with her in a rhythm that was, at once, wild and savage and glorious. It felt too good; my legs grew too weak, and they dropped from around her waist. That's when her hand lost its grip on my hip, and her fingertips traced a curve over my skin and down to my center.

"Morgan, Morgan," I panted against her, gripping her shoulders like I'd never let go. "The bedroom," I growled, arching again beneath her as her teeth nipped the lobe of my ear.

"Done," she growled back, and then she half-carried me to the bedroom.

I shut the door in a slam behind me, and then I was pressing Morgan against it, tossing the mask off her head to the floor and unbuttoning the buttons on her shirt in something akin to a single tug.

She was against the door, and I was against her, and my heart pounded, echoing around us so loudly that when she bent to trace her tongue on my neck, I thought I heard her heart keeping time with my pulse, thrumming around us, a staccato rhythm she mirrored as she scooped her hands around the small of my back, pressing me to her with such strength that it was like we were one being, the length of our bodies merging.

I tore at the offending shirt that refused to slide down her shoulders as she bit my neck, kissed my collarbone, devoured my right breast and then traced a line with her tongue to the left. I fumbled at the buttons of her leather pants as she spread her legs, drawing my hips to hers as if we were two puzzle pieces that somehow suddenly fit. I gasped as she pushed herself against me, muscles working beneath my hands as I dug my fingernails into her shoulder blades, moaning, totally and completely intoxicated by the want and need she showed me, filled with wanting and needing myself.

I tasted her skin, the soft, hot length of her neck, the curve of her shoulder, and the perfect plane and curve of her chest leading to her breasts. I cupped her breasts and bit them, twisting the nipples in my mouth with my tongue and teeth, feeling her arch against me, hearing her hiss in pleasure, feeling her hands grip my pelvis like my body was a lifeline in a raging storm that mounted all around us.

I pushed her down onto the bed as she growled. I straddled her hips, pressed myself down against her, arching my back and my face up to the ceiling as I ground down against her, as we moved together. She drew me down, and we kissed, the taste of salt on my tongue from her body.

Morgan turned me over, flipping me expertly, as if I were a doll, as her wolfish strength took over.

We moved together into the night, giving and receiving, tasting and devouring, the red of her hair cascading over my face as she crouched over me, as she pressed her lips to mine, our hearts meeting and touching and entwining together.

The moon sunk below the horizon outside, a slim smile fading from the sky.

Chapter 15: The Three Words

I triple-brewed my morning's black tea, choked it down despite the bitterness. I didn't even put any sugar in it.

"You need to stop having such loud, unfettered, glorious sex at odd hours," said Winnie, rolling her eyes at me. "*Some* of us are trying to sleep."

"Winnie, you and I both know that ghosts don't sleep," I muttered with a small smile, massaging my temples.

"Says the ghost expert!" she snorted, crossing her arms. "How do you know I don't sleep?"

I peered at her with one eye closed and a half-yawn. "You read your ghost books all night," I told her, then yawned again, this time longer and wider. "Oh, my goodness, I need to put the coffee on," I muttered, plugging in the coffeemaker.

It was just one of those mornings. One of those I-was-almost-too-sore-to-stand, I-couldn't-erase-this-ridiculous-grin-from-my-face kinds of mornings. As I turned on the coffeemaker, watching the water seep into the pot over my emergency stash of coffee, I breathed out, stared at my hands on the counter, remembered where they'd been last night. Oh, the places they'd gone, the curves they'd followed. I hugged myself tightly and rubbed at my shoulders with a smile, feeling the blush redden my face.

It was absolutely official: I wasn't falling in love with her anymore.

I'd *fallen*. Completely and utterly.

That was an odd realization, as the coffee poured into the pot, but most of the world's great epiphanies have happened over coffee. I stared at the dark liquid, immediately thinking of the Ninth Order, where Morgan was greeting customers and making drinks and laughing at a joke Victor had probably made. I felt her laughter, saw her smile when I closed my eyes and wrapped my arms about my core. I felt her, like a hand on my heart, and she was as much a part of me now as the blood that ran through my veins, as the bone that had mended where I'd broken it when I was small.

She was in my heart, and we were part of one another, in some gloriously perfect way that I still couldn't understand.

That's what love was...wasn't it? How could something so beautiful be understandable? It was warm and sure, like knowledge or tides. I pressed my hands to the counter, feeling the solidity of the formica beneath my fingertips.

I loved her.

And I needed to tell her that I loved her.

I turned off the coffeemaker. I put on a sweater. I trotted past Winnie, who'd raised her eyebrow at me but said nothing as a slow smile spread across her face. I raced out of the apartment, down the steps, and paused at the front door to the Witch Way Café as I stepped into my flats. And then I went out into the chill of an October morning, days before Halloween, bundling my hands into my sweater pockets as I felt warmth course through me.

It may have been cold outside, but my heart was as warm as an unstoppable summer.

They were setting up for the Hallow's Eve fair in the woods behind the main street of Wolf Town and its row of shops. I could hear machinery, workwomen and workmen shouting things to each other over the hubbub of metal on wood. I walked through the cacophony like it was music and approached the Ninth Order breathless as my fingers touched the handle of the door; I swung it open.

There was no one in the coffeeshop but Victor and Morgan. Victor looked up from where he leaned on the counter, reading something on his phone. He pocketed the phone, stood up with a quick smile, said something I didn't hear, and retired to the back room of the coffeeshop.

Morgan leaned her elbows on the counter and raised a single eyebrow as she smiled at me crookedly, the corners of her mouth turning up and making her face lighten. She leaned a little lower on the counter and cocked her head to the side like a wolf.

"Hello," I said, coming forward, pressing my hands on the counter, as I had at home, when I had felt so certain, when I'd known what I had to do. Faced with her eyes, faced with the smile that held the knowledge of last night, I felt weak-kneed. I took a deep breath.

"I have to tell you something," I whispered, and I leaned forward and kissed her.

Morgan was all cinnamon today, and cardamom and clove, hot spices licking along the boundaries of my mouth like fire.

"Yes?" she said, gazing at me, her eyes soft and warm, her smile just for me. When she spoke that single word, it held the world.

"I love you," I told her, the phrase sliding into the space between us, red and bright. "I love you," I repeated, as I held her gaze. "I needed you to know that I love you." I reached between us, gripping her hand tightly. "You're *amazing*. I can't believe I'm so lucky that I met you, that I fell in love with you, and I hope..." I swallowed. "I hope so much that you've been falling in love with you, too. You give me so much joy. Your very presence in my life...you..." I took a deep breath and rubbed at my eyes with my other hand as I felt tears prick the edges, grappling for the words in the book I'd borrowed from the library, the book that I'd gotten in secret, reading it in small snatches when I could. *"You pierce my soul,"* I told her quietly, leaning against the counter. It was a quote from her favorite book, from *Persuasion,* but in that moment, they were my words and only mine, and a great and powerful truth that I needed her to know.

Over the counter, she leaned again, drew me close, drew me to her like a moth to a flickering light. "I love you," she told me, then, three words that held me as tightly as she did when I kissed her. And I did—I kissed her again; I put my arms about her shoulders and drew her close, holding her to me as if she were the most precious thing in my universe.

Which she was.

I sighed, pressing my forehead to hers, feeling the thrum of her blood, feeling the thrum of mine, how they intertwined in some sort of mythical harmony, music of flesh and stardust, merging.

"I...knew you were coming," she told me then. And, completing the most solid, reassuring moments in my life, she handed me an already made latte with a wolfish grin.

I kissed her again, fiercely. Just for good measure.

My mom arrived at five o'clock exactly — as in, literally, on the dot. My phone dinged, because I — ever vigilant daughter that I am — had set an alarm for my mother's arrival, and she swept through the café's front door, along with some autumn leaves and a big boost of wind that smelled like bonfires. She was wearing her witchy best, which included her best witch hat, the black tip grazing the ceiling in the café. The coven spread out behind her, also wearing witch hats.

Since it was October and so close to Halloween, with the Hallow's Eve Fair tomorrow, everyone in the Witch Way Café assumed these ladies were in costume and applauded their arrival, as if they were about to begin a play.

Completely undaunted by the applause and expectant looks, my mom, Nancy and Sandy began a scene from *Hamlet*, with double, double, toil and troubles occupying the customers' attention for about five minutes. There was thunderous applause, then, a standing ovation from my packed diner, and then I was ushering the coven into the back room, where I could embrace them.

"The café is looking wonderful, sweetheart. Bette's going to just be so *happy* with it, and you're looking so well, too!" said Mom, going from a hug to a shoulder-length eyeball of me, and then back to a hug again. "Oh, Nan, doesn't she look beautiful? She's positively *glowing.*"

"Of course, of course," said Nancy, patting my mother's arm. "But she has customers to attend to."

"We can help!" said Sandy, with a smile.

I shook my head with a grin. "You guys are wonderful, but don't worry. I got this!" I smiled widely, pointing to the back door. "Why don't you go look at the carnival setup, and I'll be done before you know it, yeah? I close up in about an hour, so it won't take very long." They agreed, and I tightened my apron's sashes.

This had become the busiest day I'd had yet in the café. Halloween apparently brought everyone and their brother to Wolf Town, and everyone and their brother had to eat, which was very encouraging for business. I sighed for a moment, leaning against the door as I watched my mother and her friends walk through the meadow toward the woods and the carnival that was halfway set up, and I felt my smile deepen. I'd missed them, and now they were here for the best day of the year: Halloween.

Content, I went back into the café proper and took another order for flapjacks.

As six o'clock inched ever closer, the minutes began to fly faster and faster, until I flipped the sign from "open" to "closed," the glitter on the sign sparkling like never before as I said goodbye to my very last customers of the day. I closed the door behind them, hand over my heart, utter relief pooling down my spine and into the earth.

"Your aunt needs to hire someone else to help you," said Winnie, as I began to stack the dirty plates on top of themselves, balancing mugs on top of those. I laughed a little, shook my head. "We'll see about that," I told her with a smile, pushing the kitchen door open with my hip and jerking my chin toward the meadow behind the café. "Hey—can you go see if some witches are wandering around back there?" I chuckled.

She gave me a captain's salute and went to peek. I stacked the plates ever higher and transported them to the gargantuan sink at a record pace. I wondered for a fleeting moment if adding roller skates to my ensemble would make things move a little faster.

"No," said Winnie, popping her head *through* the door to the back room. "No witches."

Huh. I gathered up the last of the silverware, deposited it into the sink, and took off my apron. I didn't want to ask the obvious question of "Where could they possibly have gotten to?" because it was *my mother and her cohorts*. The answer to that question was *anywhere*.

I donned my fuzzy sweater, and, hands deep in pockets, I ventured out into the town square.

Oh, October, I thought, glancing up at the trees that rocked back and forth in the chill wind, the lights in the windows of the houses, the strings of orange bulbs tacked up along the porches. Pumpkins grinned, edging the line of the sidewalk, triangle eyes seeming to watch me as I stalked through the crunchiest of leaves. My mother wasn't out behind the shop, as Winnie had said. I wondered, for a fleeting moment, if the coven had ventured further into the woods, which I wouldn't put past them. But night was falling, the workmen were closing up shop for the day, and I didn't see my mother or her friends with them.

I stalked down the sidewalk and would have passed the Ninth Order, except that I physically *couldn't* pass it without stopping in to say hello (and kiss) Morgan. So I ducked inside the coffeeshop.

And Morgan was there, sitting at one of the larger round tables, surrounded by the coven. My mom and her friends were all chuckling at something Morgan had just said, sipping various caffeinated beverages and still wearing their witch hats. It is a truth universally acknowledged that, while average, non-Wolf Town witches can't fly on brooms, we certainly do love dressing the part of the stereotypical witch in October.

"Mom," I said, raising a single brow and placing my hands on my hips, "don't you think I'm a little old for you to be interrogating my girlfriend of choice?"

"They opted for conversation instead of interrogation, I promise," said Morgan, winking at me, eyes warm, making my knees melt just a little.

"You know, she's absolutely wonderful! I approve!" said Mom, standing, giving me the biggest, warmest hug. "I can see why you like her," she told me, nodding. And then my mother *actually* winked at me.

I'd just gotten her approval on a girlfriend—for the first time in my life.

I needed to sit down.

"Let's all go to dinner! Pizza! My treat!" said Morgan, magnanimously spreading her arms.

"Good catch on this one, sweetheart. And she's a feminist!" hissed Nan to me, as we left the Ninth Order. Her grin was as big as a sickle moon.

Chapter 16: The Fair

The next day, I knew it was time to close up the diner when I heard fiddle music.

It had been, by far, the biggest day of orders and cooking, and I was tired (well, *exhausted*, really), but all of that seemed to fade away when we heard music starting up outside about a half hour after six. Thankfully, the people that had remained in the diner paid their bills and milled out by themselves, listening to the fiddle player who began to walk through the town, listening to the woman who followed him, singing about Halloween.

I went to the café window, looked out as the fiddle player and singer passed, felt a chill travel up my spine. Her voice was haunting, his music doubly so. He was wearing a court jester outfit, cradling the fiddle to his chin lovingly, and the woman following him was dressed like a brightly colored harlequin. The musician and singer seemed to dance around one another, the one playing, the other singing her heart out, like a Pied Piper of goblins, of ghouls. They lured the people of the town (mostly in costume) to follow them, out of Wolf Town proper, out into the forest. To the Hallow's Eve Fair.

My mother and her friends had spent most of the day exploring Wolf Town, and I could see them gathering together on the sidewalk outside. I waved to my mother through the glass, and she smiled warmly at me, crooking her finger toward me. I held up my hand—*five minutes*, I mouthed—and darted upstairs to the apartment as fast as my tiredness allowed. I took the quickest shower of my life and then slowed down, reverently donning my best witch things.

A tiered and lacy black skirt went on over spiderweb tights, and I pulled on a black sweater over a purple blouse. I grabbed my witch hat (I've had it since I was a teenager, when we had a hat-decoarating party on my mother's porch and I hot-glued a bunch of spiders to it, because I was a teenager and thought spiders were cool), plopped it on my head and dashed downstairs.

I met up with the coven in front of the Witch Way Café. The lights of the shop were off, but the streetlamps and the little orange lights draped around the trees cast us all in a relief lighting of fine witchery. We were dressed to the nines and looked quite picturesque together. We posed, linking arms, when Sandy brandished her digital camera.

"All right! Let's fly, girls," said Nan

winking, even as we all groaned at the terrible pun, and we were off, out into the cool night of a Halloween delight.

In two days, it would be Samhain. I could feel the veil between worlds thinning, could feel the spirits stirring along the edges of the world, as we walked down the street, ducking out between the shops, towards the woods, following the stringed lights that seemed to make a pathway, tiki torches guttering flames, as other people fell in line.

The entire forest had been transformed. There were orange and purple and green lights everywhere, hung up so high in the trees, I wondered how anyone without wings had gotten them up there (and then realized that someone with wings probably *had* gotten them up there). Grapevine orbs wrapped in lights were suspended from varying lengths of ribbon, shining down on the brightly colored tents and booths interspersed across the forest floor. The tents were positioned in a large, rough circle. In the center of the created fair square, people in masks and elaborate costumes hula-hooped with hoops that seemed to be on fire; women ate fire off of burning sticks and spat it back out into the air, like dragons. More women and men danced with spheres of fire, poi, that swung from bright chains. It seemed that everyone swayed to the music of the fiddle player that rose all around us.

There were lovely things for sale in the tents (I spotted hand-knit socks that were luring me like sirens) and warm, mulled cider to drink, and puppet shows to laugh at and dancing to watch. I felt as if I'd gone back five hundred years, but sideways. This was not a fair from the Middle Ages but a fair from a Middle Ages that had had werewolves and magic and, you know, no pesky Black Death. My mother and the coven were delighted, but I was *bewitched*, enchanted at the man in the cat mask who walked along the little paths on stilts, towering over me; the raven girls who wore masks over their faces, and — with long, black capes — were doing some sort of complicated, whirling dance that I felt in my stomach as much as watched with my eyes.

A set of warm fingers grazed along the skin of my arm, and I turned to look. A familiar, beguiling woman with long, red hair and a crimson mask smiled wolfishly down at me.

"Hello," growled Morgan, and we embraced and kissed as the raven girls began to circle around us, the fiddler weaving his bow so quickly across the strings, I thought he might set fire to them.

"Hello," I told her, when we drew back, when the dancing had moved on from us, applause following like little birds as the dancers darted and whirled, impossible to watch without feeling vertigo.

"*This* is magic," I told her, threading my

arm through hers as she began to lead me along the corridor of tents. A woman walking in front of us wore fairy wings, and for half a heartbeat, I thought the wings actually moved, but then—I might have been seeing things.

"I'm so glad you like it," she whispered into my ear, her breath warm, spiced like cider. She tucked her own arm about my waist, then, like we were Victorian ladies strolling down a moonlit boardwalk. This was anytime and anyplace, as I felt the magic sharpen around us, delicious and full. The sky smiled down, a sickle moon drifting along the sea of stars, and all was right with this Halloween world.

Until I felt a pricking along the back of my neck. I shuddered a little, lifted my head. I saw nothing out of the ordinary for this Hallow's Eve Fair... Children laughed and chased one another; the fiddler was still plucking his strings. But, just the same, I felt a sensation along the back of my neck of being watched, and I turned in spite of myself.

"What's the matter?" asked Morgan, brows furrowed as she followed my gaze. I shook my head, composed my face, smiled up at her.

"Nothing," I told her, but it didn't sound sincere. I coughed a little.

"I'll get you some cider," she said, brushing her warm, soft lips along my forehead. In a heartbeat, she was gone, leaving a void of cold air where her warmth had been.

Again, I turned, looked over my shoulder. Again, the sensation of being watched sharpened until it was all I could feel. Admittedly, I was in the middle of a crowd of people; anyone could have been glancing at me, but it wasn't that type of sensation that I felt along the surface of my skin. And, anyway, I could see no one *actually* watching me. The laughter surrounding me, the cacophony of voices, sounded far off, distant, as a tunnel formed along my vision.

For some strange reason, at that moment, I thought about the fairies.

And then, along the edge of the woods, I saw a woman with red hair bound into a loose ponytail, a woman wearing a mask. Morgan. She was walking away into the forest.

What?

I took a couple of steps, glancing around. What was she doing? She'd said she was going to get us cider, and now…

But then, my stomach clenched as I saw what was ahead of her. The glimmer of what she had followed.

An orb of light spun in the air, leading Morgan further into the woods.

Was she bewitched? What was happening? She walked stiffly, woodenly, as if she were marching. She walked forward as if she were under some sort of spell.

It wasn't a good feeling I had as I stared after her, debating what I should do. But as I glanced around in the crowd, I didn't see anyone I knew, and, anyway, everything was happening too fast. She was moving too quickly, and there wasn't enough time.

I took off after her at a dead run, moving through the crowd as best as I was able to until I'd gotten out from the press of bodies and begun to weave between the trees, instead.

For a woman simply walking, Morgan was moving *fast*. Probably because the sphere was moving quickly, too, but she was already far ahead of me when I went between the trees.

What was happening? I hitched up my skirts and pounded across the forest floor, intent on reaching her, on grabbing her arm, on stopping her and breaking whatever spell the sphere had over her. If it even *had* bewitched her. But I couldn't think of any other reason for Morgan leaving the festivities and walking, oddly calm, collected, back poker-straight, into the forest.

Were the fairies up to something? What was going on?

Twilight was slowly fading to full-on night, and I'm not exactly the best at night vision. When I tripped over the branch, I didn't fall delicately: I landed with a very loud expletive and an *oof*.

Morgan was only ahead of me by about

ten feet at that point.

"Morgan?" I called out, panic making my word high-pitched. She'd had no reaction when I fell, when I made that sound, even though the woods were relatively quiet here, the distant festivities muted and almost silent as far out from the carnival as we'd come. "Morgan?" I repeated louder.

Nothing. She kept walking. She didn't turn around.

Something was very wrong.

I got up, then winced as I put weight down on my ankle. Great. But I'm not exactly a fainting damsel, so whether my ankle was twisted or not, I kept going, gritting my teeth together at the pain that was radiating up from my leg. But I *kept going*, anxiety beginning to build in my heart, worry consuming me. Morgan strode forward so quickly, I'd never be able to catch up with her now.

That's when I heard bells.

Morgan disappeared from view as she traveled down an edge in the land into what seemed to be a ravine. I hobbled quickly up to the edge of the bluff, crouching beneath a particularly dense pine tree. Morgan was following the orb of light into the ravine...

Where a dozen luminescent horses stood, carrying a dozen ethereal riders, wings unfurled like multicolored pennants.

It was the fairies. They'd returned.

And they'd brought their queen with them.

The queen fairy chose just that moment to stand up in her stirrups, at the head of the lot, and nod as Morgan came closer to her, still moving as woodenly as if she were a wind-up tin soldier.

I didn't know what Morgan was doing out here, or why the fairies were here (I somehow doubted it was for any sort of *good* reason), but I couldn't let her face them alone.

"Shit," I muttered then, and I got up and hobbled over and down into the ravine in plain sight.

The queen watched me impassively with her glowing eyes, her pointed nose turned up as Morgan and I got closer. I tried to hobble faster, and when Morgan finally came to a standstill, pausing right before the queen, I sighed with relief. The glowing orb darted around the queen and disappeared into her horse's satchel as I reached up and took Morgan's hand, twining her fingers with mine and squeezing tightly.

And that's when everything began to go very, very wrong.

I turned and looked at Morgan.

And it wasn't Morgan at all.

A fairy held my hand, tall and willowy and slightly terrifying with his jet-black eyes and wickedly curving mouth. I dropped his hand as quickly as if it were a live coal and had just burned me, and he chuckled a little, moving dancer-like to the only horse without a rider and vaulting up onto it.

Shit.

I'd been tricked.

"It took you long enough," came a rough voice, then.

I turned and stared, mouth open.

Allen MacRue stood on the edge of the ravine, his arms folded and his eyes dangeorusly narrowed.

"We're waiting, MacRue," hissed the fairy queen, indicating me with an impatient sweep of her hand.

I took a step backward but was surprised to find, at that moment, that the horses had moved around me.

I was surrounded.

"I have kept my end of the bargain," said the werewolf patriarch roughly; Allen would not look at the fairy queen when he spoke. "The border must be maintained, and the safeguard must remain. I give you now what you have asked for. The exchange of a soul in payment for the continued use of Wolf Town's safeguard..." And he pointed at me. "Amethyst Linden."

One fairy dismounted, and—in that moment—I understood that I was in some very deep water.

"What's happening? What are you

doing?" I hissed to Allen, who had never looked at me like that before: there was anger in his gaze, and I was deeply afraid.

"The bargain has been made," said the fairy queen, words icy and clipped. Allen, too, spread his hands with a rough shrug, not looking at me.

The fairy queen was raising her hands. I assumed she meant to do magic against me. Though I didn't know, exactly, what I'd just gotten myself into, I *did* know that I was a witch, and I would be *damned* if some sort of sparkly creature tried to out-magic *me* so close to Samhain. I closed my eyes and felt the pulse of the forest around me. I felt the energy of the fairy horses, of the fairies themselves, felt the flare of anger in Allen MacRue. I felt it all, as if from some far distance. I felt the whirl of it, the pulse of energy and magic…

And I gathered it in my heart and *tugged*…

Time slowed.

A vision swallowed me.

And I saw…

…The founder of Wolf Town, several hundred years ago, arrive to a fiercely wooded valley, felt his heart grow and grow with happiness, knowing he had found home.

…The close-minded people of the next village coming over to Wolf Town and burning down the very first settlement because they called the people there "demons" and "witches," both accusations utterly untrue, but there were no words in puritanical New England to describe werewolves.

...The founder of Wolf Town sobbing on his knees in the forest, his dying son in his arms, burned beyond repair by the fire.

...The fairies finding him in the very center of that forest and striking a deal. How they would take away the child to their realm in exchange for building a safeguard around Wolf Town so this tragedy would never happen again. That Wolf Town would always be safe if the safeguard was maintained. How, with the safeguard and the assurance of safety for all of its inhabitants, Wolf Town would thrive.

...The pact he'd made with the fairy race there, how he'd promised away his son (who was dying, anyway), and how he promised that each subsequent generation would also give a sacrifice of someone dear to the MacRue line, this person leaving his or her home on earth to live in the fairy realm in exchange for the safeguard remaining around Wolf Town.

...How the safeguard was in danger of disappearing if that person was not given over, and soon. How—if the safeguard disappeared—Wolf Town would collapse, the magic of this place disintegrating, the real world descending upon it, making every inhabitant in Wolf Town at risk of being discovered.

I opened my eyes, stared at Allen in shock, in pain, saw the pain reflected back on his own face. I felt the energy of Wolf Town, felt its almost-sentience around me, felt how many people were depending upon Allen, how much magic was dependent upon his decision. I felt so pitifully sorry for him in that moment, I didn't even know what to do.

Because I had also seen what he would have had to do if I hadn't shown up in Wolf Town. That he was wondering which one of his own kids to give to the fairies to maintain the safeguard.

That he had, eventually, decided that he was going to give himself over.

There was such loss, such pain, in that circle of trees, it froze me. I wrapped my arms about myself and shuddered. For the sake of a town, for the sake of magic, for the sake of safety for so many people who depended on him, Allen had decided to sacrifice me. Had assumed that the reason I had shown up in Wolf Town, that Wolf Town had wanted me there, was not for Morgan.

It was for this. To be the sacrifice.

"You can't," I said, and I opened my eyes. The fairies looked down at me, contempt and anger on some faces, laughter and ridicule on others. Allen's eyes were steel, and his face was set in the hardest expression I had ever seen. I curled my hands into fists, my fingernails pricking into my palms, mind racing.

And, in that heartbeat, I felt Wolf Town. I felt *all* of it, felt the great bulk of magics that it was, the diverse groupings of people and oddities and strangeness that wasn't strange at all on its streets, because Wolf Town was a shelter, a haven, a sanctuary for *people like me,* for different people, strange people who needed sanctuary, shelter…a home. And I felt the town around me and through me, and I felt it watching. Waiting.

It…wanted me to do something.

I swallowed.

I opened my eyes.

I felt her before I saw her come over the top of the bluff. But then Morgan was there at the edge of the ravine, pausing, taking in the scene before her. The look of happiness on her face melted into something questioning, and then bafflement spread across her features as she stared down at the scene before her.

"Dad…?" she called out in the quiet. "*Amy?*"

"Go back to the Fair, Morgan," said her father, still looking at me, not looking up. Morgan took a step down the bluff, and then another.

"Dad, what's going on —"

"I said *go back,*" he growled, causing the hairs on my arms to prick up.

"This needs to happen *now*," said the fairy

queen, barking it out into the cold air. "We have no more time for this nonsense. Is this the soul you give in exchange for the safeguard, Allen MacRue, or is it not?"

"*What?*" Morgan snarled, and in one instant, she was in front of me, her teeth suddenly long, sharp and bared as she stood between me and the fairies.

Between me and her father.

"*What is going on?*" she growled.

"How did you really think the safeguard was maintained, Morgan?" her father asked desperately, spreading his hands, trying to placate her. "We've had a deal with the fairies for centuries. Please don't make this any harder than it has to be. It'll be a good life that Amy has in the fairy realm. She's not dying; she's just going...someplace else." He licked his lips, and then his eyes hardened. "And you couldn't *possibly* have fallen in love with her in the short amount of time that you've spent—" But he couldn't finish his statement because of how much Morgan was growling.

"The safeguard exists because we...what, Dad? We sell someone down the river? How often do we do this?" she asked sharply. Unbelievingly.

"Once a generation," he said, his voice so quiet, it was difficult to hear him.

The fairy queen looked to Allen. "You know that if you do not make the decision now, the deal is forfeit. We will no longer protect the town, and the safeguard will die. Everyone in the world will descend upon your town, will find out what you really are, and kill you at *best*. The whole world is looking for freaks, and they will find the motherload in Wolf Town," she said with a sneer. "Is that what you want? This long legacy of safety to end with you?"

Allen's face betrayed the war going on inside of him. I was angry at him, furious, really, that he thought the reason I'd come to Wolf Town was only for a sacrifice, but I honestly couldn't understand what he must be going through. What he had gone through in order to protect himself, his family, and his town. His town that was his safe place, his sanctuary.

Morgan's hackles were raised, and her face looked half-wolf, half-woman, as she tried to control her inner wolf and not transform, the bones in her cheeks lengthening as she snarled. I could feel the anger rolling off of her in waves.

"Dad, what have you done?" she asked, her voice a low growl. Her father's hackles were up, too, and as I watched, the two werewolves began to circle one another, Morgan's eyes, now taking on a gold-flecked tone, always glancing to me.

"Don't," I whispered at the exact same moment that Morgan transformed into a wolf.

It was a domino effect—the second she

transformed, her father did, too, falling to his four paws with a great snarl as Morgan backed toward me, keeping me at her back and keeping her father and the fairies in her sights. She was still in her clothes, but they were tearing where the wolf body didn't quite fit the human-shaped clothes, the sound echoing in the stillness as the fabric ripped.

Allen's hackles rose as he snarled, his lips up and over his teeth.

And then Morgan moved forward, deadly and swift. She body-checked her father, the older wolf rolling over and over until he landed by the hooves of the fairy queen's mount.

As I watched, her father returned to his human form, kneeling and panting, hand over his heart as he shook his head. Morgan, too, returned to her human form, standing in front of me, panting.

I took a deep breath, reached forward and took her hand.

Almost instantly, she turned to look at me, and I could see the savageness in her eyes calm.

"Wait," said Allen then, raising his hand. His voice sounded tired, exhausted, and as I watched him, I saw him almost age before my eyes. I knew he was in his early seventies, but he always carried himself with a spryness and vitality. But now he looked even older than his actual age as he shook his head slowly and sadly. "I'll go," he said then, clearing his throat as he rose to his feet. "I'm sorry that I involved you," he said, taking a step toward me, and then pausing as he flicked his gaze to Morgan. "I was a fool," he said, standing tall. "I should have offered myself a long time ago. I was hoping that I wouldn't have to make this decision, and I made it out of fear. Forgive me, Morgan, Amy." He turned to the fairy queen and sighed, raising his hand to her. "I'll go," he said again.

In an instant, all of Morgan's anger evaporated. "Dad, *don't*," said Morgan, stepping forward, but I gripped her arm.

I licked my lips. Goddess, I was so nervous, but I said the only thing that was left in me to say: "Does the safeguard *need* to exist?" I asked quietly.

"*What*?" The fairy queen, Allen and Morgan said that single word at the same time. I squared my shoulders back, glancing from Allen back to Morgan.

"It was a couple hundred years ago that the town burned down, right? That someone set fire to it?" I asked, my voice weak in the beginning and then growing stronger.

"It doesn't matter," said Allen, shaking his head. "Bigotry, prejudice...they exist in any and all times. They exist now," he said, working his jaw.

"I know they do. Trust me," I said gently. "But Wolf Town is a safe place. It's out of the way of everything. There are a lot of good people here. We're stronger together, right? What if we could survive without the safeguard here?"

The fairy queen sneered at me. "It is worth the price of a single soul to save many."

"Is it?" I asked, chewing on my lower lip. I glanced to Allen, who looked pained and haunted, remembering what had happened to Wolf Town once. "I think you'll find," I said, stepping forward and placing my hand on his arm gently, "that people don't want to lose you for something that we might not even need," I said, clearing my throat.

He looked at me in bafflement. "Why are you being nice?" he asked then, tiredly. "I was going to give you to them."

"Because," I said, taking a deep breath, "Morgan came from you. And I'm pissed," I said, raising my hand. "But not enough to say that you should go with the ice queen over there," I said, jerking my thumb to the fairy queen.

"We will not come again," said the fairy queen, drawing herself up to her full height on the top of her mount. "If you forsake us, we will forsake you, and then you must live with the consequences of your decision."

"I'm a newcomer here, right?" I said quietly, holding Allen's gaze. "But I don't believe that Wolf Town summoned me. I believe

I'm *meant* to be here. That there are some things in this universe that you can't explain, and that being in the right place at the right time is one of them. This safeguard may have kept the town safe, but Wolf Town itself is full of people who are strong and good, and who can help each other if close-minded people come our way. No one's going to find out about you guys being werewolves, or about the vampires or the lake monsters, and even if they do, who would believe them? All I'm saying," I said with a sigh, "is that there's no reason for you to sacrifice yourself. We can deal with the fallout if there is any. Together." I squeezed Morgan's hand, and she squeezed back.

"Dad," she murmured, her voice low. "We can do this. We don't need the safeguard. We've been doing pretty well without it lately. It's been flickering," she explained when her father raised his head and glanced at her skeptically. "The safeguard's been flickering a lot, actually," she finished. "Don't do this. Don't give yourself over to them. End this right now. I never knew that this was part of our family history," she continued. "But it needs to end today."

"I've kept my silence for so long," her father said then, brokenly. "For so long, I've tried to do the right thing..."

Morgan stepped forward and affectionately, tenderly, gathered her father into her arms and hugged him tightly. "It's all right, Dad," she said, her voice soft. "It's over."

Morgan turned and glanced at me, holding out her hand. I took it again, and again, the two of us stood together, shoulder to shoulder, as we stared up at the fairies.

"We are no longer in need of your services," said Morgan coldly. "Leave Wolf Town," she intoned. "And do not return."

As I watched a million reactions and emotions flit over the fairy queen's face, as I watched Morgan's father turn away from the fairies, as I watched Morgan, this beautiful werewolf woman, stand defiantly, her face upturned to the fairy queen on her luminescent mount, I was afraid, yes, of what the fairy queen would say.

But I was prouder, by far, of Morgan. That fierce pride and love poured through me, and I squeezed her hand tightly. I saw the generations of the MacRue clan shifting as I held her hand, as I watched her father turn away, as I watched her make that decision. I knew then that Wolf Town would eventually be Morgan's to help, to protect, to keep safe.

And mine, too.

And all of ours.

"Farewell," spat out the fairy queen, and they were all gone in a flash, like they had never been there.

Morgan sagged against me, and I

wrapped my arms tightly around her, brushing my lips against her cheek.

"You did the thing I never had the strength to do, sweetheart," her father said gently, with a deep sigh. "Thank you."

Around us, I could feel the last bits of energy of the safeguard evaporate. But that was all right. Already, I could feel the vibrancy of the town behind us, could feel the vibrancy of the Halloween festival already in full swing, full of amazing, strange, weird and wonderful people who would band together, who would, in the coming days, reach out and help one another more than ever before.

"We're wolves, Dad," said Morgan then, quietly, flicking her intense, green gaze to me. "We're not afraid of anything," she said, squeezing my fingers tightly.

We walked back to the Halloween festival, the forest around us silent and dark...but I walked with the wolves.

I was in love with a wolf.

And I wasn't afraid.

Epilogue

The old Town Hall seated about a hundred people. Which was about how many townsfolk there were in Wolf Town.

Which meant that, on Halloween night, the Town Hall was *packed*.

Morgan stood in front of everyone, explaining the fact that the safeguard had been eliminated, and what that would mean for the town. That we'd have to be careful if we were "different" from most humans. That, perhaps, if we were werewolves, we shouldn't transform (or hunt) outside of city limits. That we should be respectful of the neighboring towns, but that, at the end of the day, we shouldn't be afraid.

And the townsfolk listened to her with rapt attention. And though there were a few naysayers, for the most part, everyone applauded the fact that they were no longer dependent on a safeguard that had been built several centuries ago.

And then we spent a good hour discussing how to transport Ellie's lake monster children to the ocean. It was a full Town Hall agenda. And a practically normal subject for Wolf Town.

It was a little odd having a conversation with Allen afterward. I knew it was going to be awkard for a while. He had, after all, intended on making me a sacrifice. That was bound to ruin any sort of beginning relationship. But I only had to see him at holiday dinners, probably, and that was all right. We'd avoid each other and talk about the weather when we couldn't avoid each other. It'd be like a normal family holiday dinner.

After the Town Hall meeting, Morgan and I went out into the chill air of Wolf Town. The sun was setting along the edge of the horizon, the leaves were roaming across the main street of the town, and the air smelled deliciously of cider and pumpkin. We walked, arm in arm, past the Ninth Order and Victor locking up for the night. He gave us a toothy grin and a nod and slipped the key into the lock. We walked past the Witch Way Café, where my aunt, Bette, freshly arrived back from her vacation, was locking up, too. She flashed me a grin and a thumbs-up sign. And a pretty bawdy wink. I was growing to really like her; she was just as crazy and wonderful as the rest of my family, and I was still helping her out at the café part-time.

We walked all the way to the end of the main street of Wolf Town, to the final building on the left, a brick building that had stood for over two hundred years.

And, on the top floor, was Morgan's home, her condo.

Our condo now.

"You realize that we're making all of those terrible lesbian U-Haul jokes a reality, right?" I asked her, as I laughed when she picked me up, ready and willing to carry me across the threshold.

"You didn't use a U-Haul," she growled reasonably, glancing down at me with a seductive little smile. "So we're stereotype-free."

"Right," I whispered, my heart pounding inside of me as she set me down just inside the door.

"These are strange days for Wolf Town," said Morgan seriously, her brows furrowed. "I know it's all screwed up, what my father did. I'm sorry, again, Amy—"

"Shh," I told her, pressing my finger to her mouth. "I don't *care* what your father did," I said, and then shook my head at her protest. "I really don't. He was trying to do the best he could for the town, and, anyway, he didn't succeed in giving me over to the fairies, did he?"

"No," she said, her voice low. "But he almost did. I almost lost you..." She trailed off, wrapping her fingers around my hips, holding me close to her.

"But you didn't," I said, placing my arms around her neck and holding her gaze. "I'm right here. I'm staying," I whispered, standing up on my tiptoes, "right...here..."

"I love you, baby," she said, her mouth soft and warm and lingering as we kissed, as my wolf ate me up, like they warn in all the fairy tales. I kissed her back just as deeply, though, holding her closer, tighter, stronger.

She was my wolf now, and forever.

"Come on," said Morgan, one sexy brow raised as she kicked the door shut gracefully behind her. She chuckled at me, a low and throaty laugh, and she kissed me again. "Let's make this a *happy* Halloween," she whispered.

And we did.

The End

If you enjoyed *Wolf Town*, you'll love Bridget's Sullivan Vampires.

The following is an excerpt from "***Eternal Hotel***," the first novella in the Sullivan Vampires series, a beautiful, romantic epic that follows the clan of Sullivan vampires and the women who love them. Advance praise has hailed this hallmark series as "*Twilight* for women who love women" and "a lesbian romance that takes vampires seriously! Two thumbs up!"

...So *this* was the staircase from last night, next to the front desk. The Widowmaker. It must be. I'd never seen a steeper set of stairs. From up above, they looked simply like the rungs of a ladder in a barn—so steep and so tall and almost impossible to even think of taking.

It's not that I don't like heights—I'm pretty okay with them. But these stairs were something else. I wasn't taking these steps—I'd have to circle back somehow and find the other spiral staircase down to the first floor

As I turned, I caught the first floor out of the corner of my eye. Because of the cathedral ceilings of that first floor, it seemed much farther away then I'd thought it was.

It was then that something strange happened.

The ground seemed to spin under me for

a moment, bucking and heaving like I was trying to walk on waves of carpeting, not good firm floor. Or did it really? Was it just a trick of the eye? Either way, I took a step backward as a shadow fell in front of me, but there was no floor beneath that foot stepping backward, then, and I was *tumbling* backwards, shock cold enough to burn me flooding through my body as, impossibly, I began to fall down the stairs.

A hand caught my arm. I hung suspended over the abyss of the air, my back to the emptiness, and in one smooth motion, I was pulled back.

Saved.

The hand was cold, and the body I brushed against as I was hauled out of the air felt as if the person had stepped out of a prolonged trip through a walk-in freezer. I looked up at the face of the woman who had saved me, and when I breathed out, I will never forget it: my breath hung suspended in the air between us like a ghost.

She was taller than me by about a head, and I had to lean back to gaze into her eyes. They were violently blue, a blue that opened me up like a key and lock as she looked down at me, her eyes sharp and dark as her jaw worked, her full lips in a downward curve that my own eyes couldn't help but follow. She wore a ponytail, the cascades of her silken white-blonde hair gathered tightly at the back of her head and flowing over her right shoulder like frozen water falling. She wore a man's suit, I realized, complete with a navy blue tie smartly pulled snug against her creamy neck. She looked pale and felt so cold as her strong hand gripped my wrist, but it was gentle, too. As if she knew her own strength.

I saw all of this in an instant, my eyes following the lines and curves of her like I'd trace my gaze over an extremely fine painting. And, like an extremely fine painting, she began to make my heart beat faster. That was odd. I was never much attracted to random women, even before I dated Anna, even before Anna…well.

But this wasn't just my heart beating faster, my blood moving quicker through me. This was something else. A weightlessness, like being suspended in the air over the staircase again, the coolness of her palm against my skin a gravity that I seemed to suddenly spin around. When she gazed down into my eyes, she held me there as firmly as if her hands were snug against the small of my back, pressing me to her cool, lean body that wore the suit with such dignity and grace that I couldn't imagine her in anything else.

I was spellbound.

She said not a word, but her fingers left my wrist, grazing a little of the skin of my bare forearm for a heartbeat before her hand fell to her side. I shivered, holding my hand to my heart, then, as if I'd been bitten. We stood like that for a heartbeat, two, the woman's eyes never leaving mine as her chin lifted, as her jaw worked again, her full lips parting...

"Are you all right?" I shivered again. Her voice was dark, deep and throaty, as cool as her skin, as gentle as the touch of her fingertips along my arm. But as I gazed up at her, as I tried to calm my breathing, my heart, we blinked, she and I, together.

I knew, then.

I'd heard that voice before.

I'd seen this *face* before.

"Have we...met?" I stammered, eyes narrowed as I gazed up at her in wonder. We couldn't have. She shook her head and put it to the side as she looked down at me, as if I was a particularly difficult puzzle that needed solving. I would have remembered her, the curve of her jaw and lips, the dazzling blue of her eyes. I could never have forgotten her if I'd only seen her once. It would have been impossible.

I took a gulp of air and took a step back again, unthinking, and her hand was there, then, at my wrist again as she smoothly pulled me forward, toward her.

"The   stairs,"   she   said   softly, apologetically. I'd taken a step closer to her this time, and there was hardly any space between us, even as I realized that my hand was at her waist, steadying myself against her. I took a step to the side, quickly, then, my cheeks burning.

"I'm sorry," I managed, swallowing. "And...thank you..." Her head was still to the side, but this time, her lips twitched as if she was trying to repress a smile.

"I've been meaning to remodel these steps. Not everyone knows how steep they truly are," she said, and her lips did turn up into a smile, then, making my heart beat a little faster. I took a great gulp of air as she held out her cool fingers to me, palm up.

"I am Kane Sullivan," she said easily, her tongue smoothing over the syllables as the smile vanished from her face. "You must be Rose Clyde," she said gently, the thrill of her voice, the deepness of it, the darkness of it, saying my name, the way her lips formed the words...I nodded my head up and down like a puppet, and I placed my hand in hers. Her fingers were *so cold*, as she shook my hand like a delicate thing, letting her palm slide regretfully over mine as she dropped my hand with a fluid grace I had to watch but still couldn't fully understand.

I was acting like an idiot. I'd seen beautiful women before. But Kane wasn't beautiful. Not in that sense. She was...compelling. Her face, her gaze, her eyes, an impossibility of attraction. I felt, as I watched her, that buildings, trees, people would turn as she walked past them, unseeing things still, somehow, gazing at her.

I knew her, then.

The painting. The woman in the painting from last night, with the big, black cat, lounging and regal and triumphant and unspeakably bewitching. The naked woman, I realized, as my face began to redden, warming beneath her cool, silent gaze. She was the woman from the painting. But as I realized that, as we silently watched one another, I realized, too, that that would have been impossible. It had been a while since college, it was true, but I could still tell when a painting was a few hundred years old.

The woman in the painting could not possibly have been Kane Sullivan. And yet, it couldn't possibly have been anyone else.

"I'm...I'm sorry," I spluttered, realizing — again — how much of an idiot I must look to this incredibly attractive creature. Her lips twitched upward again, and her mouth stretched into a true smile this time, the warmth of it making the air around her seem less frozen.

"You're fine. It's not everyday that someone completely uproots their life and charts a course for places unknown," she said, turning on her heel and inclining her heard toward me. As she turned, I caught the scent of her. Jasmine, vanilla...spice. An intoxicating, cool scent that was warm at the same time.

Unmistakable and deeply remarkable. Just like her. I stared up at her with wide eyes as she gestured gracefully with her arm for us to walk together, like she was a gentleman from the past century. True, she was wearing a sharp man's suit (that I was trying desperately not to stare at or trace the curves of it with my eyes—and failing), but there was something incredibly old fashioned about her. I kept thinking about that at that first meeting. Like she was from a different era, not the one of smart phones and the Internet and fast food french fries. No. The kind of era that had horse-drawn carriages, corsets and bustles and houses that contained parlors. We began to walk down the corridor together, in the opposite direction I had come, me sneaking surreptitious glances at her, her staring straight ahead.

The spell of the moment was broken, but a new spell was beginning to create itself, weaving around the two of us as we walked along the corridor. As she spoke, I stared half up at her, half down the hall stretching out in front of us. All of my actual attention, though, was on this woman.

Every bit of it. She was just like that. So...compelling. She was a gravity that pulled me in, hook, line and sinker. I didn't know then how much of a gravity she had yet to become to me.

Acknowledgements

I wrote *Wolf Town* while Natalie and I planned our wedding together. I remember writing the last sentence about two days before our actual wedding day. Writing this novel kept me sane during the whirlwind and fast-paced joy that planning our wedding brought us. Revisiting the novel now, it has brought me much of that same joy in the form of memories. So these acknowledgements would be incomplete without thinking of every single family member and dear friend who came to our wedding, supporting us with their love. Getting married when you're a lesbian is sometimes a difficult endeavor, and the love shown to us at our wedding erased some of the hardships we underwent in order to have our perfect day free of homophobia. Thank you, from the bottom of my heart, to our beloved guests and bridesmaids, sweet ringbearer and flower girls, and to our officiant, who performed his first *legal* gay marriage with us in our state! It was a life-changing day, one I cherish.

P.J. Bryce is incredibly supportive of my work and everything I try to do in this world. I'm so grateful that my best friend is also a writer, and I'm so grateful for the thousands of hours of conversation we've had together outlining the finer points of werewolf pack hierarchy and laughing together. I'm blessed to know you, and extra blessed that you always tell me what you love and don't love about a story I'm cooking up. I wouldn't be half the writer I am without you, so thank you for everything.

Marian and Ruby are two of the most wonderful women I've ever met. Natalie and I both are so incredibly grateful for your friendship and support in all of our publishing and writing endeavors, and all of our crazy life adventures. We love you both fiercely.

This book is especially dedicated to Terri, who is really awesome beyond words. Who else would tell me how to use a Stanley knife and cut drywall? I'm so lucky I met you—you're a wonderful friend, and I'm grateful for you.

I am eternally grateful to every single person who buys my books, who reviews them or cheers me on as I'm writing them. My fans and friends are some of the best in the universe—I'm so grateful for you. You make all of this worthwhile. Thank you from the bottom of my heart. :)

And to the love of my life. Natalie, I don't know what I did to deserve you. You are my soul mate and the best thing that ever happened to me. I love you, baby. Thank you for sharing this wild adventure with me. Life is beautiful with you beside me.

CPSIA information can be obtained
at www.ICGtesting.com
Printed in the USA
LVHW111555050220
645950LV00001B/287